I0728665

A NOVEL BASED ON THE LIFE OF

FILIPPO BRUNELLESCHI

BUILDING
HEAVEN'S CEILING

Joe Cline

The Mentoris Project
745 Sierra Madre Blvd.
San Marino, CA 91108

Copyright © 2018 Barbera Foundation, Inc.
Cover photos: juriskraulis/istockphoto.com
                alex_so/istockphoto.com
Cover design: Suzanne Turpin

More information at www.mentorisproject.org

ISBN: 978-1-947431-10-2

Library of Congress Control Number: 2018935685

All net proceeds from the sale of this book will be donated to the Mentoris Project whose mission is to support educational initiatives that foster an appreciation of history and culture to encourage and inspire young people to create a stronger future.

Publisher's Cataloging-In-Publication Data
(Prepared by The Donohue Group, Inc.)

Names: Cline, Joe, author.
Title: Building heaven's ceiling : a novel based on the life of Filippo Brunelleschi / Joe Cline.
Description: San Marino, CA : The Mentoris Project, [2018]
Identifiers: ISBN 9781947431102 (paperback) | ISBN 9781540167712 (ePub)
Subjects: LCSH: Brunelleschi, Filippo, 1377-1446--Fiction. | Architects--Italy--History--To 1500--Fiction. | Santa Maria del Fiore (Cathedral : Florence, Italy)--Design and construction--Fiction. | Church architecture--Italy--History--To 1500--Fiction. | LCGFT: Biographical fiction. | Historical fiction.
Classification: LCC PS3603.L554 B74 2018 (print) | LCC PS3603.L554 (ebook) | DDC 813/.6--dc23

The Mentoris Project is a series of novels and biographies about the lives of great men and women who have changed history through their contributions as scientists, inventors, explorers, thinkers, and creators. The Barbera Foundation sponsors this series in the hope that, like a mentor, each book will inspire the reader to discover how she or he can make a positive contribution to society.

Contents

Foreword

First and foremost, Mentor was a person. We tend to think of the word *mentor* as a noun (a mentor) or a verb (to mentor), but there is a very human dimension embedded in the term. Mentor appears in Homer's *Odyssey* as the old friend entrusted to care for Odysseus's household and his son Telemachus during the Trojan War. When years pass and Telemachus sets out to search for his missing father, the goddess Athena assumes the form of Mentor to accompany him. The human being welcomes a human form for counsel. From its very origins, becoming a mentor is a transcendent act; it carries with it something of the holy.

The Mentoris Project sets out on an Athena-like mission: We hope the books that form this series will be an inspiration to all those who are seekers, to those of the twenty-first century who are on their own odysseys, trying to find enduring principles that will guide them to a spiritual home. The stories that comprise the series are all deeply human. These books dramatize the lives of great men and women whose stories bridge the ancient and the modern, taking many forms, just as Athena did, but always holding up a light for those living today.

Whether in novel form or traditional biography, these books plumb the individual characters of our heroes' journeys. The power of storytelling has always been to envelop the reader in a vivid and continuous dream, and to forge a link with the subject. Our goal is for that link to guide the reader home with a new inspiration.

What is a mentor? A guide, a moral compass, an inspiration. A friend who points you toward true north. We hope that the Mentoris Project will become that friend, and it will help us all transcend our daily lives with something that can only be called holy.

—Robert J. Barbera, President, Barbera Foundation
—Ken LaZebnik, Founding Editor, The Mentoris Project

Chapter One

"There was once a day I believed a funeral shroud would be the only clothing I would ever wear," said Brunellesco di Lippo, as he scrutinized his appearance in a mirror encased by a golden frame. With fingers covered in jeweled rings, he adjusted the finely spun silk garments on his torso, then opened his topcoat to reveal an inside lined with chiffon-colored mink fur for all to see.

A man of little height, Brunellesco turned his heels inward to examine his narrow-tipped leather shoes. He had paid the cobbler for a custom-made high heel discreetly built into the sole. After pondering for a brief moment, he decided the shoes were worth the price and reflected on his past, "I remember waking up barefoot on the stone floor of that one-room house where I was born many years ago in Lippo, near Bologna. The wooden planks were a pathetic attempt at being a wall, and the wind howled angrily through the open gaps. The bitter cold lashed against me, leaving my skin raw. Though I wanted to return to the safety of my slumber, I couldn't.

"Shivering with each step, I approached the scant light dying in the earthen hearth. No heat was given off; only despondence and despair radiated outward. And as I stood reflecting upon the squalor of my life, another gust of wind assaulted that wretched house. Looking down at the hearth, I noticed the coals were as black and dead as my future would be were I to stay there.

"My stomach growled for subsistence. But all I had was moldy bread. When I close my eyes all these years later, I can still see the maggots thrashing about as I caught them. I needed at least six for just a meager mouthful of bread. But even as I forced the toughened leather down into my gullet, my efforts were futile. Within seconds, my stomach contents regurgitated themselves on my tattered clothes."

Brunellesco's son, a rambunctious eight years old, Filippo Brunelleschi, judged every word with great skepticism, saying, "Mother, I don't remember this part of the story."

An exceptionally tall woman, Brunellesco's wife, Giuliana, tugged an embroidered sleeve past her wrist then hushed her son. "Be quiet, Filippo, and let your father finish his story."

"You too, Giuliana. It's my story. I was there. Were any of you there?" asked Brunellesco sharply.

Giuliana relented. "Filippo and I are sorry. Please continue, husband," she said placatingly.

Brunellesco continued, "That's what I'm trying to do... So, there I was covered in excrement when the door opened. A floral aroma overwhelmed my senses. I looked up to find the plague doctors entering. Their elongated masks reminded me of a vulture's beak. Both rely upon death for existence. But as they began to circle, I would not allow death to happen to me."

"So, are you no longer just a notary, Father, but an immortal as well?" interrupted Filippo.

"Filippo, do you wish to dine with the dogs on the floor tonight?" asked Brunellesco.

"Possibly, Father," answered Filippo.

"Keep talking, and your wish shall be granted…Back to my story. They wanted me dead, but I ran away from that plague-ravaged city and took with me nothing except my boyhood dreams of something better. I found myself outside the city walls for the first time unsure where to go, so I simply walked away from where I did not want to be. The minutes passed into hours and those hours became days. Time elapsed and so did my energy until Heaven shone her grace down upon me in the form of a she-wolf, who nursed me back to health."

Giuliana glanced skeptically at Brunellesco. "A she-wolf, husband?" she asked.

"Were you there? It was a she-wolf," proclaimed Brunellesco.

Filippo whispered to his mother, "Now, was Father Romulus or Remus?"

A hushed giggle escaped from Giuliana's lips.

Her husband rolled his eyes in frustration. "Should I just stop telling you my story?"

Giuliana replied, "I just remembered last summer during the heat wave when Filippo tried to shave the dog. Poor little *cucciolo*, we never saw him again. I mean, please continue, husband."

After clearing his throat, Brunellesco continued, "When I first gazed upon Florence from afar, I believed my mind was playing tricks on me. Surely I was ill as never had I seen so many people in one place. And they were all alive. Back in Bologna I had seen such numbers, maybe even more. But they were all dead and buried in a mass grave."

"Please don't give Filippo nightmares," reprimanded Giuliana.

"I tell Filippo this every year, so he doesn't forget our past. So many youths of today have forgotten their roots. They simply amble along, blind to where they came from and unsure of where to go. I do not want our children growing up like that."

Filippo interjected, "Children? You mean *child*, for I do not see Cassandra anywhere."

"Your older sister went to the tailors to pick up our Easter scarves," replied Giuliana. "Now, Brunellesco di Lippo, my dear husband, please continue with your annual punishment…eh, I mean annual tradition."

Filippo forced his mouth closed to prevent any laughter from escaping.

"Not only were the Florentines I saw alive, but they were laughing," continued Brunellesco. "Never had I heard such vociferous laughter. Back in Lippo, the Black Death not only took lives without hesitation but stole any notion of happiness, laughter, wonderment…Simple delights were all pilfered from those who survived. All those little things so many of us simply take for granted.

"The early morning sun was at my back as I splashed through the stream outside of the eastern gate. Nerves made me tremble walking through such a daunting structure. It towered over me, and I remember it nearly stretching up to the clouds. But then the city's commotion washed over my senses. I was overcome by the vendors hawking their wares noisily and potential customers examining everything with cautious eyes. It was like it happened just yesterday.

"And as I ventured deeper into the city, the crowds grew greater and larger in number. Eventually, I was unable to move through the walls of people. And it was there, with nowhere to go, that I gazed upward and first saw it dominating the cityscape: Santa Maria del Fiore! All these Florentines were gathering for an event there, and I was determined to find what it was and be a part of it.

"Being a small boy, I was fortunate I could eventually navigate through the endless sea of people without much resistance and found myself in the Piazza del Duomo. Bells soon rang out from the heights of Giotto's Campanile, sending a spark through the crowd. Moments later, the grand doors opened at Santa Maria del Fiore and all those in attendance filed into the cathedral. I joined the flow of the crowd and soon was staring into the largest building I had ever seen. And that day was Easter, just like today."

Brunellesco di Lippo and Giuliana's oldest child, Cassandra, opened the massive wooden door leading into their abode and stood on the threshold wearing two long, finely woven scarves. Fortunately, she had not inherited her father's features; instead, she took after her mother and was long and lean. "I apologize for taking so long," Cassandra said as she searched for an excuse. "The tailor had to finish them."

"Whatever you say, dear sister," said Filippo. "Father, now that Cassandra has joined us, would you mind retelling your story from the beginning? I know she just loves hearing it so much. It truly is one of her favorite parts of the year," he said as Cassandra glared at him.

Brunellesco di Lippo walked to the door. "Come, children, we must get going to Easter Mass. But don't fret, Cassandra, for I shall start at the very beginning, just for you."

Cassandra responded hesitatingly. "It truly is fine with me, Father. You can just start wherever you left off upon my return," she said.

"Nonsense," he assured her. "It is important for both of you to learn that these walls around and ceiling above us did not just appear from out of nothing. It took years of working hard and studying, which allowed me the chance to become a notary. And you know what I did after that? I worked even harder."

As they set off, Filippo Brunelleschi hurried ahead of his family on the crowded streets of Florence's San Marco district. Giuliana cautioned him not to stray too far, but he outran her plea.

Brunellesco placed a hand on his wife's shoulder. "Let him have his fun for now. He is a boy, and boys need to do such things. He'll tire himself out."

Giuliana pointed to multiple construction projects around their path and said, "Something could happen to him. What if someone drops a hammer or a brick?"

Brunellesco responded, "Today is Easter and even construction halts on this day. Much like it did all those years ago in my youth."

Not amused in the least, Cassandra interrupted, "We know, Father. You first came to Florence on Easter."

"But do you know what happened next?"

Giuliana crossed her arms, saying, "Those conducting Easter Mass saw a dirty boy and took pity upon that little clump of dirt and hair."

"And all of that occurred on this very day, many years ago," Brunellesco said, smiling. "Can you either of you believe that?"

Noticing Cassandra's growing frustration, Giuliana said, "Could you bring your little brother back, please?"

Cassandra exhaled with relief. "Yes," she said, then hurried off after Filippo.

"But don't you want to hear how I excelled in school?" asked Brunellesco.

Giuliana placed her hand on his chest. "Let her be, husband. But you can tell me again for the millionth time."

Filippo wove his way through the slower Florentines, then he heard his sister's voice calling somewhere from behind, "Filippo, come back here!" she said.

"You must catch me first!" retorted Filippo.

He sped up, darting through the streets. When turning back to see where Cassandra was, Filippo ran into a wooden cart pulled by an ox and his forehead struck a sharp corner. The jarring impact knocked him to the stone pavement.

Cassandra ran over to Filippo on the ground and asked anxiously, "Filippo, are you all right?"

As the surrounding crowd hovered curiously, Filippo stared up in a state of confusion. He blinked rapidly, trying to regain his senses. Beneath his forehead blood pumped to the injured area, forming a massive swollen bruise within seconds.

When his parents realized that it was their son on the ground, they rushed to him with great concern. Giuliana cradled her son's head. "Filippo, what on earth did you do?"

"He ran into the back of a cart," explained Cassandra. "I saw the entire episode. If you ask me, he deserves what happened."

"Now is not the time, Cassandra," snapped Giuliana.

Brunellesco knelt down to his son's level and asked, "Do you feel all right, Filippo?"

"My head hurts," answered Filippo.

"You ran headfirst into a cart. You should be worried if it didn't hurt." Brunellesco smiled, which immediately comforted the boy.

His worried mother held up two fingers. "Filippo, how many fingers do you see?"

"I see two."

Giuliana relaxed, saying, "It appears nothing within his head got damaged."

Brunellesco helped Filippo back up to his feet and told him, "Let me know if you do not feel like attending Mass, and I will escort you back home and entertain you with how important this day is."

"Husband, be careful, your stories might induce more damage in our youngest," insisted Giuliana.

"Nonsense. Well, Filippo, what would you like to do?" asked Brunellesco.

Without any hesitation, Filippo continued on his way. "Mother is right. Let's hurry to Easter Mass before we are forced to stand in the very back."

Giuliana looked at Brunellesco. "This day is quite special, for I never thought your stories would actually serve a purpose," she said cheekily. Brunellesco responded with a sarcastic laugh and a toss of his head.

Standing out in the Piazza del Duomo, Filippo looked up from the shadow of the Santa Maria del Fiore. Each time he rested his eyes on the enormous cathedral, the impressive sight of the Gothic architecture left Filippo speechless and awestruck. He approached the exterior walls rising high above the surrounding buildings and reverently traced the marble sides with his fingers, marveling at the mosaic composed of a myriad of whites, greens, and pinks. Brunellesco appeared behind him and said, "Do not touch, Filippo. Remember, this is not just a building. This is a work of art for Florence. A work of art where Florence worships."

With a height of over two hundred feet, the basilica dwarfed both father and son as they walked along its eastern side. However, the quintessential symbol of Florence had not always been such. An earlier cathedral had been erected nearly a millennium before the fifth century in honor of Saint Reparata. Born in the third century, she was arrested by Roman authorities in Palestine for her Christian faith. Despite being submitted to grueling torture, she would not forsake her faith. Her defiance enraged her Roman persecutors, and they sought to make an example of her. According to lore, she was sentenced to burn at the stake; however, through divine intervention it rained that day, extinguishing the flames. But Reparata did not receive a reprieve. Instead, her jailers increased the torture and forced her to drink searing-hot pitch. Again, Reparata defied her captors and refused to yield her Christian beliefs. Her staunch defiance in the face of Roman authority eventually resulted in her beheading. Though her body was subjected to physical death, Reparata's unwillingness to compromise her beliefs would become the stuff of legend. Cities across Christendom would venerate her with monuments, as displayed in fifth-century Florence.

Over the centuries, time slowly weakened and eroded the ancient cathedral of Saint Reparata. By the late thirteenth century, efforts were under way by Arnolfo di Cambio to redesign the cathedral. But di Cambio would not live to see his design completed because he died in 1310. A few short years later, members of the Wool Merchants' Guild took over the project's patronage. Their collective efforts reignited efforts to finish the cathedral. To help ensure completion, they hired the Florentine architect Giotto di Bondone to lead the construction project. His efforts achieved di Cambio's vision, but like di Cambio, Giotto would die before the cathedral was completed in 1337. His successor, Andrea Pisano, continued to work on the basilica until 1348, when the Black Death arrived in Florence. This scourge would cause all construction to cease for over a year. When the Black Death subsided and freed the Italian city-states from its lethal grasp, Florentines immediately went back to work on the cathedral. Three years after the birth of young Filippo Brunelleschi in the year 1380, the nave was finished. But the massive ceiling of Santa Maria del Fiore remained incomplete; the ceiling was open to the sky, exposing those below to the elements.

Filippo followed closely behind his father into the interior of Santa Maria del Fiore. Entering through the doors, he was led into the marble structure that epitomized the Gothic style. A vaulted ceiling, supported by equally tall stone columns, stretched to the unfinished ceiling situated above the nave. Below, throngs of Florentines filled every open space in an attempt to show their religious devotion on this holiest of days. From the richest to the poorest, every level of society was present on that day.

With the service about to start, Brunellesco scoured the crowd then turned back to his son. "Do you see your mother or sister anywhere?"

Filippo stood up on the tips of his toes but was unable to see over those in attendance. "No, Father, I do not."

"We shall just have to meet up with them after Mass," said Brunellesco, taking Filippo by the hand. "We shall stand where I did those many years ago. Feel free to make your mother and sister jealous of such an honor."

Relunctantly following, Filippo sarcastically responded, "Oh, yes, they will certainly be green with envy…like turtles."

~

The closing words of the Latin Mass echoed through Santa Maria del Fiore. Lost in the crowd, Filippo was unable to understand a single word before turning his attention instead to the basilica's structure. His tilted his head back and stared up at the massive open space. To his surprise, snowflakes slowly began to flutter down over those leading Mass. Filippo tugged on his father's arm. "Father, why is there an opening? Wouldn't it have been better to enclose the entire cathedral to shelter us?"

Brunellesco looked at his son. "Do you remember the story of Icarus and his wings?" he asked the boy.

"Yes, Father. He tried to fly with his waxwings fashioned by his father. But he got too close to the sun, and his wings melted."

"Exactly, Filippo. And so did all the architects who built this place. They sought to achieve the grandiose and sublime through their work. And they clearly *did* meet that goal in some regard. But their ambition was too much. When they realized their mistake, it was too late to be rectified. And the unfinished ceiling is a constant reminder to all us Florentines to understand our limitations. We should find the limits and learn not to exceed them."

"Do you think that someone might be able to complete it?"

"The greatest builders of the past and of our time have all tried, and all have failed."

With resolve burning his eyes, Filippo continued to stare at the open space.

Brunellesco grabbed him by the arm. "Come, we need to try and find your mother and sister."

Chapter Two

No longer a boy but a young man of eighteen years, Filippo Brunelleschi walked out of the doors of his prestigious *abaco* school into the Florentine sunlight. Over the past few years he had toiled, acquiring a lay education consisting of mathematics, rhetoric, Latin, grammar, and history. His scholarly efforts paid off when Filippo finished at the top of his class. The folded parchment clutched in his hands provided the evidence of his academic success.

The sunshine illuminated the relief on Filippo's face at the knowledge that he had completed his primary schooling, but this was quickly replaced with an impending sense of dread. Reality hit him hard in the solar plexus and brutally forced the air from his chest. Filippo stumbled forward on rubbery legs before dropping to his knees on the cobblestone pavement. He slowly collected his wits while still on the ground, murmuring, "I can do this."

While Filippo gave himself a pep talk, a nearby donkey brayed at him. He locked eyes with the annoying ungulate and yelled, "*Stupido* donkey! Do not mock me! I can do this!"

But the donkey disagreed and brayed again in his direction.

Filippo stood up and walked to confront his tormentor but realized a rope tied around the donkey's neck kept it restrained. An evil grin widened across Filippo's face and he began taunting the donkey. "Look at you, donkey, with your ugly long face, like the bastard of an ugly horse and an ugly pig."

The donkey snapped his mouth towards Filippo. "Do not even try me today, beast. See this?" He waved his graduation parchment in front of the donkey. "It says I'm smarter than you, *stupido* donkey." But Filippo was too close and the donkey grabbed the parchment with its teeth. "That's mine!" exclaimed Filippo. "Let go!"

The two engaged in a tug-of-war for control of the parchment when a voice screamed out, "What are you doing to my donkey?"

With a final yank Filippo freed his parchment from the donkey's grasp, then addressed the owner, "Your stupid beast was trying to eat my education!"

Filippo stood outside the expensive Carrara marble exterior of his family's house. Ever since the creation of the Roman Republic, Carrara marble has captivated sculptors and builders alike for its durability and unique hazy white coloring highlighted with subtle veining. It took a dozen quarrymen working for Brunelleschi's father over six months to remove the solid mass of marble. The next year was spent dividing the marble into more manageable but still massive bricks. These bricks were transported by ship down the Italian coast to where the Arno River empties into the Mediterranean. Dozens of horse-drawn carts carried the bricks to their journey's final destination, Florence, where Brunellesco di Lippo would construct his palazzo, one worthy of himself. He believed that if Roman emperors enjoyed this marble, there was no reason why he should not.

Now his son stood in front of the family home, his fist clenching the donkey-chewed parchment. He struggled to gulp down air. As a boy, his father used to frighten him with stories of how the marble bricks had claimed half a dozen lives during the quarrying and transportation. Refusing to be the house's seventh victim, Filippo turned to walk away. But the sturdy oak door opened revealing Filippo's father, Brunellesco, standing in the threshold. With pride, he asked "Filippo! I've been waiting all day for your return. And how did you do?"

Filippo extended his arm and offered the parchment. Brunellesco took it in his hands and unfolded it. But disgust flashed across his face as he pulled his hand away covered with drool. Noticing the unusual dental imprints of something not human, he asked, "Did a horse chew on your academic parchment, Filippo?"

"No, Father. It was a donkey."

"A donkey?"

"It was an insulting donkey that mocked me and then wanted to eat my education," insisted Filippo.

"Is that why you are late in returning?"

Filippo stood there in utter silence. Brunellesco took his silence as a nonverbal affirmation, then returned his attention back to the parchment and commented, "Wonderful. Your grades speak for themselves. I promise there are no mocking donkeys in my line of work. There are numerous jackasses, but no donkeys." Brunellesco searched for a smile on his son's face but he could not find it. "Come, let's go inside."

Filippo followed glumly behind his father like a man walking to the gallows.

Inside, surrounded by an interior of dark chestnut, Brunellesco asked, "Why are you so solemn, boy? Are you sad about no longer being the baby?"

Filippo looked up at his father, "Has she given birth yet?"

"Not yet, but she's about to burst."

Aided by Cassandra, a pregnant Giuliana waddled into the room, visibly close to the end of her third trimester. "I hope sooner than later. How did you do, Filippo?"

Brunellesco handed her Filippo's parchment. "He made us proud parents."

Giuliana hugged Filippo. "You know you're of age to follow in your father's footsteps." She placed her hand on her stomach. "I think the baby's kicking."

Cassandra pointed at a wet spot increasing in size on Giuliana's robe. "Mother, have you had an accident?" she asked innocently.

"I guess the baby heard me," said Giuliana, right before a bolt of labor pain sent her reeling to her knees.

Brunellesco dropped to her side. "Cassandra, Filippo, you two get a midwife immediately."

Filippo nodded his head in response. "Yes, Father."

Later that night, Filippo and Cassandra sat in a room by themselves waiting to hear word on their mother's condition. Cassandra looked at Filippo and said, "You seem so distant. Are you sure it's not about losing your place as the youngest?"

Filippo stared back with certainty. "It is not that, I assure you."

"I know what it is."

"Feel free to guess all you want, older sister, but you will not understand," said Filippo.

Cassandra pondered for a brief moment then responded, "You just finished with primary schooling; now you must apprentice with Father to one day inherit his company. But you do not want to do that, do you?"

Her words stunned Filippo. It was as if Cassandra had read his thoughts and knew his innermost fears. "Cassandra, are you a witch?" he said, surprised. "Are you in league with the devil? If you are, I am telling Mother and Father. You are going to be in so much trouble!"

Cassandra shook her head in disbelief. "I'm not a witch, nor am I in league with anything supernatural. But do you honestly think you are the first child in the history of time to feel such a way?"

Filippo stammered a reply, "Yes? Maybe? No?"

She said, "I felt the same thing, especially after being informed of my expected duties for the family."

"Which are?" asked Filippo.

"To marry up for our family, just as you will carry on the work of the family."

"But I don't want to," proclaimed Filippo.

"Do you think anyone cares about what you want, Filippo? Our lives were planned for us before we were born. And you will become a notary. Then you will get married. Then you will die. That will be your life."

Filippo protested, "You may have accepted your destiny, but that does not mean I will too and accept our parents' expectations like a man kneeling at the executioner's block."

Brunellesco rushed into the room. "Please come meet your new little brother!" he said excitedly.

"And Mother?" asked Filippo.

Brunellesco smiled. "Ask her yourself."

Because of the high rate of infant mortality, the clergy had decided upon a mandatory two-week period of waiting before an infant could be baptized. It was during that time that most parents worried over their child's health, but not Brunellesco and Giuliana. Their youngest son, Modesto, had been showing them he was quite alive through his ceaseless crying during the day and especially at night.

As the entire family walked through the streets of Florence, Brunellesco and Giuliana showed all the signs of their sleepless nights upon their faces. Giuliana was holding Modesto, adorned in a bundle of maroon silk, when he began to cry. "There he goes again," said Brunellesco. "Do you think after the baptism gives him a soul, he will finally quit wailing like a wounded beast?"

"Wounded beast? Really, Brunellesco? He's probably hungry. I can't remember if I fed him this morning," wondered Giuliana.

While Giuliana prepared to breastfeed, she passed off Modesto to Cassandra, who examined her little brother and asked, "Were Filippo or I ever this bad?"

"You two rarely ever cried," Brunellesco responded.

Giuliana adjusted Modesto to feed him, then interrupted her husband. "Don't listen to him. Both of you cried, not nearly as much as this one, but you did."

"I don't remember them crying at all," stated Brunellesco.

"That's because you were at the office working late into the night," said Giuliana.

As the family turned a corner, they entered the Piazza del Duomo and the Baptistery of St. John, the epitome of Florentine architecture, swung into view. The minor basilica was built upon a Roman palace on the same site from an initiative put forth in the eleventh century to redo and expand the religious building with construction finishing in 1128 AD.

Brunellesco directed his family, saying, "Let us enter from the east."

As they walked by Santa Maria del Fiore, Filippo looked at his father, shocked. "So, you are superstitious now?" he asked.

"Not any more than the next man. However, I do enjoy looking at the panels."

"What are you talking about, Father?"

"Look for yourself. All the doors except for the eastern doors are unadorned."

On the two massive bronze doors, the life of St. John the Baptist was depicted on twenty-eight intricate gilded panels that took the artist, Andrea Pisano, six years of painstaking effort to design. Filippo stared at the great work and said, "Father, why do you think only these doors have panels?"

Brunellesco shrugged at the question. "Probably ran over budget or something. But imagine if they had not," he replied.

Filippo motioned up to the open roof on the Santa Maria del Fiore. "Imagine if they, too, had a bigger budget."

"Son, certain things in this life can be accomplished. Bronze doors like these are one thing. However, finishing a dome of that size is nothing more than a distant dream in a far-off land," said Brunellesco, as he led his family through the bronze doors into the octagonal building.

Inside the limited space they approached their places with silent reverence, but walls of white and green patterned marble inlay initially attracted Filippo's attention. However, it was the gold mosaic on the ceiling that captivated him. Masterful stonework told visual stories of Jesus, Joseph, St. John the Baptist, and the Last Judgment. As his little brother was being baptized, Filippo's head remained fixed on the amazing architecture.

After the ceremony was over and they were back out in the piazza, Brunellesco sighed with relief. "Well, the little one's got a soul now. That's a good thing."

Giuliana cradled Modesto in her arms. "He was quiet the entire time. Maybe that was all he lacked?"

Brunellesco patted Filippo on the back. "I will be returning to the office in the morning. I think that will be a perfect time for you to start learning the ropes of my profession," he said.

His father's words froze Filippo in place. Eventually, he found the courage to speak up. "I will not be joining you in your office."

Brunellesco's face betrayed his emotion. His brow furrowed with anger upon hearing Filippo's response. He flapped his hands angrily in the air and yelled, "What do you mean you will not be joining me?!"

With a deep sigh, Filippo told him the truth, "I am to report for school."

"School? You have had enough school."

Holding Modesto in her arms, Giuliana stepped in front of Filippo to defend him from Brunellesco. "It has already been arranged, husband. Filippo will start attending goldsmithing school in the morning," she said.

"What does Filippo know about goldsmithing? He has never even held a hammer!"

Giuliana spoke. "My uncle worked his connections on Filippo's behalf. Our son's grades seemed to impress them enough for acceptance," she said.

Brunellesco stared down at Filippo disdainfully. "A farmer knows how to farm. A doctor knows how to heal. I gave you the best education that I could to ensure your future success as a notary. When I was your age, I would have jumped at the chance for such an opportunity. But you have decided to throw everything away. Everything I worked for all those late nights, to give you all those chances that were never given to me. And this insolence is how you repay me?"

Filippo looked down at his feet, afraid to look up at his father.

"Can you not hear me, Filippo?" demanded Brunellesco, and with an open hand he slapped his son across the face. The force knocked for Filippo to the ground.

Giuliana handed Modesto to Cassandra, saying, "Hold him." She interjected herself between her husband and son and said, "Brunellesco, that is enough!"

Furious, Brunellesco stormed off. Giuliana helped Filippo up to his feet. "I'm sorry for suggesting that you tell him after Modesto's baptism. I thought he would be in a generous mood."

Filippo rubbed his face to soothe the pain and said, "He was quite generous with his anger."

Giuliana comforted him, saying, "Your father just expected certain things from you, being the eldest son and all."

Filippo motioned to Modesto. "He's now got another son that he can raise to be just like himself."

Later that night, Filippo lolled in a chair carved from dark-grained walnut wood and adorned with soft calf leather. Though glittering tapestries filled the walls around the room, he concentrated on a raging fire burning in the marble hearth. He focused upon a log, watching as flames slowly consumed it.

From out of the shadows, Brunellesco appeared with a bowed head. "I wanted to apologize for my actions earlier."

Though the words startled Filippo, he did not let it show and continued to stare into the flames. His father stepped around the chair Filippo sat in and walked toward the hearth. He extended his hands and flashed his palms in an apologetic manner. "I wanted to ask forgiveness for what I did today. I overreacted. And that was not right."

Filippo sat back in the chair and listened to his father's words, which provided more warmth than the fire.

"I never knew you did not want to succeed me."

"I did not want to disappoint you," said Filippo.

Brunellesco let his son's words steep in the silence. After a moment, he realized what his son meant. "And I do not want to disappoint you by making you do something you resent. You are an adult now, Filippo. Your decisions must be and can only be made by you and no one else. Do you understand what I'm trying to convey?"

With a nod of his head, Filippo signaled that he understood.

Brunellesco turned his attention to the fire. "Do you really think this is something you can succeed at?"

With fiery resolve in his eyes, Filippo answered, "Goldsmithing requires creative problem-solving in design. Such physical riddles appeal to me much more than being a notary."

Brunellesco turned back to his son. "And gold is quite a precious resource."

Chapter Three

FLORENCE, 1396

The next morning, Filippo Brunelleschi pushed off a goose down comforter and linen sheets, then sat up in bed. Light from a newly risen sun crept in through the bottom corner of a window that looked out onto Florence. Within moments, light flooded into his room. Filled with hope and brimming with unbridled optimism, he bounced out of bed ready to face the day.

In the kitchen, Filippo found his father finishing breakfast. Brunellesco placed a bowl of porridge down on the table, stood up, and addressed his son. "Good morning, Filippo. I must get going, but I bid you good luck." Walking out of the room, Brunellesco stopped and cast back a stern look over his shoulder, then said, "Remember, if this is truly the path you want to take in life, don't let the small failures accumulate and deter you from your calling."

Filippo responded cheerily, "That is why it is school, a place where we learn not to make mistakes. It is where we fail in order to succeed in the real world."

"Yesterday, I found myself in the study oblivious to the world, reading about the exploits of Philip II of Macedonia," said Brunellesco, "and his son."

Filippo interrupted, "So, who impressed you more? Philip II or Alexander the Great?"

Brunellesco smiled. "I'm glad your schooling did not fail you, nor my wallet. I found both to be rather fascinating. But I was left curious as to whether Alexander would be remembered for being great if it were not for the tutelage of Philip II."

"Despite expanding his empire, didn't Alexander the Great die at the old age of twenty-seven? Was that part of his tutoring as well?" asked Filippo.

Brunellesco shook his head at his son's disrespectful question and walked away just as Giuliana passed by. Entering the kitchen, she hurried to remove fresh loaves of bread from an open oven. As the bread cooled, she stepped over to a boiling cauldron, removed a ladle from within, and filled a bowl with steaming porridge. Placing the bowl in front of Filippo, she said, "You have a big day today, son. Eat."

Filippo protested, "I'm not hungry."

"But you soon will be. In time, we always get hungry."

Filippo dragged a spoon through the porridge before placing a spoonful into his mouth. He turned to his mother and said, "There. All full."

Giuliana glowered at him and said, "Keep going."

Under his mother's watchful eye, Filippo force-fed himself porridge. After eating another few spoonfuls, he pleaded, "Can I just go to school?"

Satisfied, Giuliana nodded her head. Filippo stood and hurried out of the room, but she yelled, "Here, take some bread in case you get hungry later."

"Will you ever take a 'No' for an answer?" asked Filippo.

"Do you?" quipped Giuliana while handing him two loaves of bread. She gave him a hug and said, "Have a good first day."

From a nearby room, Modesto cried, and his screams floated into the kitchen. She turned to that direction. "Guess your little brother's up." But Filippo was already gone.

Somewhere down an ill-lit Florentine alley, Niccolo di Betto Bardi stood upright with rigid fury in his faded, wrinkled clothes. The glimmering silk suggested that they had been expensive and trendy at some point in the recent past. He unleashed a boisterous rant to a teenage boy cowering at his feet. "Where is it, you worthless brat?!"

His son, Donato di Niccolo di Betto Bardi, simply Donatello to friends, turned himself over on the filthy ground and insisted, "Father, I did not take your wine! Do you hear me?! I did not take your wine!"

Niccolo kicked Donatello in the rib cage, shouting, "You better have not!"

Donatello picked himself up off the alley floor onto a knee and said, "Did you not hear me?"

Niccolo answered his son by charging at him and pinning him against an alley wall. He gripped Donatello by his shirt, clenched his fist, and buried his knuckles into his son's chest. With minimal effort, Niccolo lifted Donatello up off of the ground, locked eyes with his son, and snarled, "You fancy yourself a sculptor, do you, boy?"

Niccolo's free hand grabbed Donatello's wrist and pinned it against the alley wall by nearly punching through it. With the utmost seriousness, he said, "If you took my wine, Donatello, I will take a hammer to your hands and will not rest until every bone is flattened. You have my word." He then dropped Donatello against the wall and walked away.

With his head buried between his knees, Donatello refused to look anywhere other than down at the grimy alley floor. When he finally did look up, his face streamed with tears and he fought to control a quivering lip. As Donatello rested his cheek on his knee, he realized someone was standing at the alleyway's entrance.

"Are you all right?" asked Filippo, as he stepped into the alley.

"I can breathe, and I can still use my hands. I am more than fine," responded Donatello, who turned away from Filippo and his question.

Filippo nodded his head and said, "Very well," and continued on his way. A few steps away, he remembered the two loaves of bread his mother had given him that morning. Filippo pivoted around, but when he returned to the alley he found no one.

Since the tenth century, the vaulted arches of the Ponte Vecchio have risen out from the Arno River to support the shops above. Maintaining the bridge's structure is integral to the welfare and safety of those living and working atop the Ponte Vecchio, but more importantly for the Florentine economy as a whole. For within the bustling shops above the river's surface, merchants exchange gold, the lifeblood of Florence.

Filippo walked with haste on the Ponte Vecchio when church bells rang in the distance, signaling the hour. As he realized the time, he felt very fearful. He started running, but the busy crowds on the streets of Florence refused to yield to him. An unseen elbow hit Filippo and sent him to the ground, where he narrowly avoided being hit by a cart. As he collected his breath on the floor of the Ponte Vecchio, he remembered his class and jolted up.

Wiping the dirt from his clothes, Filippo muttered, "*Meraviglioso*. I'm not just late now, but I look like I rolled in a pigsty."

Standing in the doorway to the Accademia di Orafi, Maestro Alano Umberto greeted the entering students as if each were a long-lost friend. Filippo arrived at the end of the line and waited behind other potential fellow goldsmiths. He soon stood before Maestro Umberto, who eyed his disheveled appearance. "You're lucky that for goldsmithing the final product is judged by its appearance and not by the appearance of the producer."

Filippo sheepishly apologized, "I'm sorry, Maestro."

Maestro Umberto closed the doors behind Filippo and said, "At least you made it here today," then turned his attention to the entire class. "But come tomorrow, I will not be able to say that for everyone here."

The students looked at each other with uncertainty, when a loud bang on the door attracted their attention. The noise even surprised Maestro Umberto, who turned around and opened the door to reveal Donatello.

"May I help you?" asked Maestro Umberto.

Donatello searched for an excuse. "There was an accident with oxen and other assorted farm animals. But I made it."

Maestro nodded his head. "Very well. Please join everyone else." Upon his words, Donatello made his way over to the rest of the class.

After clearing his throat, Maestro Umberto addressed those in attendance. "As I was saying, not all of you will be back tomorrow. I find talent is not an innate quality within all. It is not within most. It is within the very select few. Some may toil away for hours, days, and weeks. And as those weeks drift into months, all those months become years. And during that entire time, progression in one's talent might occur through diligence, work ethic, patience, commitment, and whatever other nonsense you have been taught since suckling at the breast of your wet nurse. But here at the Accademia di Orafi, we do not have the luxury of time to help your artistic pursuits grow and flower. You are not plants requiring water. You are all men and will be treated as such. And because of that, half of you will be gone by tomorrow. Today, all of you will be handed an equal amount of tin to work. At the end of the day, your work will be judged against the work of your classmates."

Maestro Umberto's hand disappeared into a velvet satchel on his waistband and removed a nugget of gold. The students gathered around the glistening metal as Maestro Umberto continued, "This shiny little rock is the reason you all are here. For this, countless lives have been extinguished far sooner than before their time. Battles and wars have been waged to fill chests up with this rock. But what I do as a master goldsmith along with my guild brethren is *create*. And it is our craft's creations that explain why there is such a fateful desire for a mere shiny rock."

He reached into another satchel on his waistband, but this time revealed a ring with an intricate pattern carved into the band. "As a goldsmith, your work will take the valuable and make it priceless. Out of earthly metals, you will craft objects worthy of only the divine." His fingers pulled out a golden cross with an assortment of inlaid jewels. Rubies, sapphires, and emeralds, each intricately cut and polished, filled the crucifix's interior. With a gleeful look on his face, Maestro Umberto chuckled, "Of course, that depends on how one defines the divine."

With the entire room captivated, he continued, "Ancient Egyptians believed the sun was a chariot forged from gold that traveled across the sky. Upon Mount Olympus, Greek gods only wore clothes sewn from golden thread. Surely you all are familiar with it being one of the gifts presented by the Magi to Christ upon his birth. When we see it, we see purity of light. But it is this same purity that can lead men astray through corruption and greed. It is important to distance yourself from the medium of a goldsmith and general opinions of gold. It is now important to place gold above even your own lives. Over at the wood carver's workshop, do you think anyone cares about the pile of excess wooden scraps on the floor? As a goldsmith, you better believe people care about that scrap of gold on the floor, much, much more than they care about your lives."

Maestro Umberto scanned the room, checking to see if his speech had made an impact on his students. He pouted with disappointment walking up to the front of the room, then turned back to the class. "Are any of you familiar with King Midas?"

A single hand rose up; it belonged to Filippo. Maestro Umberto grinned. "At least one of you does. Please tell the rest of your class about him."

Filippo cleared his throat, then said, "He was a Greek king who wished all he touched to turn into gold. But he turned his daughter to gold, so he washed his hands to get rid of the gift that he had."

Maestro Umberto nodded in approval, then added, "Whereas King Midas had gods to help him realize his mistake, all your prayers will go unanswered today. Now let's discover which one of you has the hands of King Midas."

After leading the students into a workshop with a large open kiln in the middle, Maestro Umberto distributed the same weighed amount of tin to each student. Filippo examined the amount in his hand, then took his spot at a workbench. He eyed the various instruments organized atop the workbench: two different-sized calipers, a wide hammer, a narrow hammer, a rabbit's foot for polishing, metal wire, and multiple chisels ranging from tent stakes to needles.

Maestro Umberto's voice broke Filippo's concentration. "Each of you will also be given a space around the kiln. I will be assisting in that part to hurry things up. You may begin now." He flipped over a waist-high hourglass, and a stream of sand trickled downward.

All the students encircled the kiln like hungry wolves ready to start—everyone, that is, other than Filippo. Instead, he retrieved a piece of paper and a piece of charcoal. Before touching the charcoal to the paper's surface, he contemplated what to draw while rotating the tin with his fingers. When inspiration hit him, Filippo treated the charcoal like an extension of his hand. His arm moved in wild and rapid strokes as if he were conducting a symphony on the paper.

Maestro Umberto helped a student remove molten tin from the kiln, but his eyes focused on Filippo, still sitting by himself at the workbench. When most students returned to their workbenches, Filippo flipped over his drawings, then walked up to the kiln. "Are you ready?" asked Maestro Umberto.

Filippo replied, "For this stage, yes."

"This stage?"

"You'll see."

The immense heat from the kiln quickly turned the tin into a malleable state. Maestro Umberto instructed, "Be careful so that you may live to see the next of your stages!"

Filippo returned to his station and carefully turned over his drawing while still shielding it from any prying eyes. He grabbed a hammer and a chisel and began separating the searing metal. Every few seconds, he would check and compare his work against his multiple drawings, each showing various angles of a rose with a falling leaf. After rolling the stem with a hammer's handle, Filippo picked up the smaller of the two calipers and snipped away at the tin with extreme precision and care. His movements pinched and pulled the tin out from the stem, thus creating the appearance of thorns.

Maestro Umberto looked at the sand in the hourglass, which appeared as if about half the sand had fallen. Loudly, he said, "Everyone put down your tools!" Then he placed the hourglass onto its side to stop sand from falling any further. "Some of you might want a break. Here it is." He revealed a much smaller hourglass and flipped it upside down, saying, "Some of you might not want a break and may want to continue working. If you gain entry into my school, I will applaud such effort. But for now, no one will receive any advantage."

The students stood up and filed out of the room. Filippo folded his drawing and hid it in his waistband. With his blueprints safe, he retrieved the two loaves of bread from beneath his workstation. Heading for the door, Filippo checked again to make sure that his drawing was secure.

Outside the Accademia di Orafi, Donatello sat on the stone wall overlooking the Arno River. Filippo approached him from behind, holding out a loaf of bread. "Would you like some?" he asked.

Donatello turned around with agitation and said, "Are you talking to me?"

Although traffic was heavy along the Ponte Vecchio, no one else was around them. Once again, Filippo offered the bread. "My mother baked it this morning with fresh wheat gathered from the countryside."

Donatello looked at the bread, then asked, "Did I see you this morning?"

Without hesitation, Filippo responded, "Yes. I saw you in the workshop. We're both trying to be goldsmiths."

"Exactly. What were you drawing earlier?"

Filippo handed Donatello a loaf of bread. "Hold this," he said, then retrieved the folded blueprints from his waistband.

Donatello bit off a mouthful of bread, then studied the intricate design. "Will you be able to accomplish this?"

"We shall both find out by the end of the day."

Impressed, Donatello complimented Filippo, "Your drawings, I've never seen anything like them."

"Do you not plan your approach?"

"Plan my approach? I simply look at it and do whatever comes naturally."

"I was brought up to believe that if you fail to plan, you plan to fail."

"We'll see if your plan grants you the chance to stay. In the meantime, would you care for some wine with your bread?" asked Donatello, brandishing a bottle.

Filippo accepted the bottle and took a gulp. "Thank you, my friend. My name is Filippo Brunelleschi." Donatello shook Filippo's hand while guzzling the wine. After wiping the excess wine off his face, Donatello let out a thunderous burp then said, "I'm Donato di Niccolo di Betto Bardi, but everyone calls me Donatello for short."

The kiln had been running all day so the workshop now resembled a sweatbox. Students choked on the thick air as they toiled on their projects. Filippo returned to his workstation with a tray holding little dots of heated tin. He used the hammer to flatten the dots. For some, he took the metal string and made light indentions into each dab. Holding a caliper in each hand, he pinched the end of each and slightly twisted them. The result created realistic-looking leaves and petals that fluttered in a slight breeze.

As Filippo compared his progress to his drawings, Maestro Umberto walked over to his work. Once satisfied with a position, Filippo attached each leaf with great precision. His movements reflected a patience and skill far beyond his years. When he stopped to wipe the sweat off his brow, Filippo noticed that Maestro Umberto had moved on to other students; Filippo returned his attention to his work.

On a nearby workbench, Donatello worked in a drunken stupor, occasionally punctuated by loud burps for which he refused to apologize. He used a thin chisel to push in on a flat sheet of tin, then reached for his bottle of wine. He held it over his mouth, but nothing came out. "*Merda!*" he yelled as he threw the empty bottle against the wall.

Everyone stared at Donatello, who shrugged it off, saying, "What? I drank all the wine. What else would you do if you had no more wine?"

Donatello returned his focus to the tin panel. Though his fingers were callused and dirty, the object he held was beautiful. It depicted the biblical story of Jesus raising Lazarus from the dead. Subtle folds in the tin created the illusion of shadows cast on the crowd gathered around Jesus. Maestro Umberto studied Donatello's technique and said, "I have heard some talk about your natural abilities, but I must say your talent might surpass those murmurings."

"Murmurings? I let my talent speak for itself. And it yells from the highest peaks of the Alps, deafening all who hear it."

"Such raw emotion. If you can harness it, you could be one of the greatest."

"And who says I'm not already?"

"You have the ego of a great one in the making," said Maestro Umberto patiently.

A voice erupted with urgency from the far side of the workshop. "Maestro Umberto! We need help!"

Maestro Umberto hurried over to find students surrounding a young teenage boy, passed out from the heat. Umberto knelt down and checked the boy's pulse, saying, "He's still alive, but his dreams of being a goldsmith are dead like he will soon be unless we get him out of here. Any volunteers?"

The students returned to their work at an increased pace. Only Filippo raised his hand to volunteer. "There's one extra set of hands," said Maestro Umberto. After surveying the rest of the class, he reached his decision. "Donatello, would you mind giving us a hand?"

"No, Maestro, I do not mind, but first," he said, searching his body for something. Spotting a pile of broken glass, it dawned on him. "Oh, that's right, I already drank that bottle." He stumbled his way over to help Maestro Umberto.

Maestro Umberto barked instructions at Filippo and Donatello. "Each of you lift up a leg. I've got his arms." They squatted down and each grabbed a leg when a loud shriek filled the workshop. Maestro Umberto glanced at a student running around in circles waving a flaming arm. "Christ Almighty! It's only the first day, and one of them has already caught fire!" he exclaimed.

Maestro Umberto picked up a wooden pail filled with water and walked over to the burning student. "Stay still, now," he said. Closing one eye so as to aim better, he flung the water directly onto the student's burning arm, thus extinguishing the flames. "That was a close one," sighed Maestro Umberto, but noticed Filippo and Donatello still standing around the student. "Oh, he should have been taken out of here a while ago. You two do that while I take care of Prometheus here."

Donatello walked up to the student's upper body and made eye contact with Filippo, saying, "I'll grab up here, and you grab his legs."

Together, they grabbed tight fistfuls of cloths and lifted the student. Though his limbs were in the air, the student's lower back was curled and dragging on the ground. Struggling, Donatello commented, "He's heavier than he looks."

With Filippo leading the way, they blundered through the classroom. Navigating around the room, Donatello accidentally slammed the student's head into the leg of a table. "Good thing he's not awake, right?"

"Hopefully, he will wake up after that."

As they walked out the door, Donatello began to lose his grip on the student but before he could say a thing, the fabric slipped out through his fingertips. The student's head bounced off the stone floor with a dull thud.

Donatello smirked. "He and his dreams of goldsmithing are now one and the same, for they are both dead."

Filippo laughed as they set the student down on the surface of the Ponte Vecchio.

Back inside in the workshop, Maestro Umberto smeared healing salve over the student's charred arm. He handed the salve to the student and said, "Make sure to apply this constantly, or they'll have to cut your arm off." The words terrified the student but Maestro Umberto turned his back on him and left the room.

Lost in the haze of the workshop, a young man immersed himself solely in his work. Not once had he lifted his head up, despite the surrounding chaos. And even during the break, he smuggled out tin in his pocket to polish. Ever since he was little, Lorenzo Ghiberti had been constantly told that he was a genius who was destined for greatness. As the son of an accomplished goldsmith, Ghiberti had been honing his craft even before he could speak in full sentences.

When Filippo and Donatello returned to the workshop, they noticed that the others were huddled around something. They quickly joined the fray to see what was capturing everyone's attention. Filippo made his way up to the front and realized that Ghiberti was the center of attention, then he returned to his work. In doing so, he accidentally bumped into Ghiberti, causing Ghiberti to make an error in crafting the tin. Filippo realized he was at fault and quickly apologized, "I'm sorry, friend. I did not mean to do that."

Ghiberti spun around in a rage and said, "How dare you try to sabotage my greatness, you talentless hack!"

Filippo stared, bewildered by Ghiberti's anger. "There was no premeditation nor ill will on my part, friend."

"Don't call me friend, for I am not! When it concerns you, I am the furthest thing from such a trivial relationship!" yelled Ghiberti, pushing Filippo to the floor.

Maestro Umberto stepped between the two men and said, "Lorenzo Ghiberti, what Filippo did was a mere accident. No different than what one expects when at a crowded marketplace."

"Accident? An accident he forged out of jealousy over my talents," spat out Ghiberti in a rage.

Ghiberti glared at Filippo and charged. Before Filippo realized what was happening, Ghiberti had punched him in the face.

The impact initially stunned Filippo and he felt a burning sensation on his nose. Unsure if his nose was still there, he inspected it with his fingers. Blood trickled down from his nostrils onto his fingers. Maestro Umberto examined Filippo's bruised face and said, "You should wash the blood off your face." Then he turned his attention to Ghiberti and said, "If you do such a thing again, you will be gone. I don't care how talented you might be. Goldsmiths should fight with their talents, not with their fists."

Ghiberti found the words audacious, so he stared back at Maestro Umberto and responded, "Do you know who my father is? Or do I need to show you my family name like I did to that inept, filthy hack?"

Filippo rinsed the blood off his face with water from a pail. Anger raged within him. Without hesitation, he rushed across the workshop, dove at Ghiberti's legs, and lifted him off the ground. Carrying Ghiberti over his shoulder for a few steps, Filippo slammed him down onto the workshop floor. Amidst clouds of soot and dust, Filippo sat on Ghiberti, straddling his torso and throwing a steady stream of punches and headbutts. Immediately, students pulled him off of Ghiberti, who continued to cower on the ground.

Maestro instructed both Filippo and Ghiberti to stand up and coldly said, "Both of you are dismissed for the day."

"But what of our work?" asked Ghiberti.

Maestro Umberto answered, "I will judge each of your work as it currently is. Now, leave my workshop and learn not to act like barbarians."

Ghiberti stomped his way to the door while mumbling a long string of expletives. Filippo turned to follow him out, but Maestro Umberto placed a hand on Filippo's shoulder and said, "Someone's been needing to put that pompous brat into his place. I only wish it were with your skills and not your fists. But beggars cannot be choosers, now can they?"

Filippo apologized, saying, "I'm sorry for my actions."

"Why? Don't be," responded Maestro Umberto. "If you are to make it in this craft, you must learn to throw a punch when the situation calls for it. Or else no one will respect you for your art. Do you understand, Filippo?"

Filippo understood, but his head flopped in despair. Dragging his feet toward the door, he contemplated all his mistakes. With one foot out the door, something urged him to look over his shoulder and in that brief moment, Filippo caught Maestro Umberto leaning over his workbench to inspect his tin rose.

With his dreams dashed, Filippo walked out to where the lively merchants plied their trade. He wandered north of the Ponte Vecchio through the winding streets of Florence, spotting Giotto's Campanile rising high above the cityscape. Bells rang out from the tower, the melodious chimes wafting through the air. Filippo walked toward the tower like it was a warm fire on a cold, dark night.

Filippo stood below in the shadow of the Giotto's Campanile when the echoes of the ringing bells drifted off into silence. His attention turned to the Santa Maria del Fiore. "Will both our dreams remain unfinished?" he wondered.

In the day's little remaining light Filippo shuffled across the Piazza del Duomo, scattering a group of pigeons into the air along the way. Unbeknownst to him, Donatello had seen him leaving the piazza. Tired and sweaty, Donatello placed his hands on his knees to catch his breath and muttered, "Damn it, Filippo. I hope this will be worth it. But that was some damn good bread."

Back at his house, Filippo walked in feeling melancholy. He was so despondent he forgot to close the front door and simply sank to the ground. Giuliana's voice called from another room, "Is that you, Filippo?" She wandered into the entrance hall and said, "How was your first day?" then noticed him slumped over on the floor.

Filippo looked up with watery eyes and said, "It's over. All is lost."

Giuliana spotted the remnants of a bloody nose and yelled, "Brunellesco! Filippo got attacked!"

Brunellesco ran into the entrance hall. "Filippo, what happened?"

Filippo turned to his father and spoke, "You were right all along. About everything."

A knock on the open door broke the silence. Standing in the threshold, Donatello asked, "Is Filippo home?"

Brunellesco pointed to his son on the ground and stated the obvious, "There he is."

Donatello exclaimed, "Filippo, you made it!"

Filippo wiped the tears from his eyes. "What?"

"Maestro Umberto approved of your work. You were officially accepted," responded Donatello.

"Really?"

"I'm not going to say it a third time, but yes."

Giuliana rolled her eyes and said, "You had me worrying there. But it appears you gained entry to school, and you made a friend."

"Not just a friend, but one left in amazement at eating your homemade bread," interjected Donatello.

Giuliana smiled. "At least someone enjoys my cooking. Please, Donatello, sit and eat with us. But only if you keep complimenting my cooking."

Chapter Four

FLORENCE, 1402

After crossing the Adriatic Sea, defeating Gentius the King of Illyricum, and seizing full control of his lands in 168 BC, Roman soldiers discovered a gold vein in an area in the south. In 10 AD Augustus ordered the province of Illyricum to be divided into two provinces, Pannonia in the north and Dalmatia in the south, partly to protect Roman financial interests in the Dalmatian mines. Over a century later, slaves used metal pick axes to break into the stone ore and reveal a particular gold vein. Ships transported the gold to Rome, where it was melted down into Roman coins bearing the face of the Roman Emperor Trajan. He used these coins to purchase the allegiance of barbarian tribes to the north of Italy. But if any tribe refused, they would meet the might of Imperial Rome in the way of the professional soldiers who comprised their military. A man of legendary pragmatism, Trajan knew that baskets of gold coins could help alleviate the suffering of his enemies.

Most of the gold coins would be lost over time. However, one coin journeyed back to Rome, where a merchant discovered it hidden inside an ancient clay vase, almost as if it had been hidden by its last owner. The merchant returned to his home in

Florence and it was there that Maestro Umberto first laid eyes upon the glimmering gold coin. The reflected light reminded him of a warm Tuscan sunset in late summer. He remembered very clearly asking the merchant, "Whatever it costs, I must have this."

The intense heat of a furnace warped the golden coin into a bubbling liquid, then steady hands carefully poured the searing metal into the top of two similar-looking molds. "Now we wait," said Filippo.

Donatello removed a cork from a wine bottle. "Correction, my friend, now we drink."

Filippo accepted the bottle and took a drink. Donatello asked, "How long until the gold sets?"

Filippo handed the bottle back to him. "The only thing remaining is to plunge them," he said.

Together they each submerged a mold into a trough of water with the aid of giant calipers. The heat immediately vaporized the water and filled the room with steam. Filippo pulled his calipers out of the water. "Time to see if this worked."

Donatello set his mold on a table and said, "This is your work, so you can open your own mold. If anything is cracked, I don't want to be blamed."

"Fine, my friend, for it will be my individual success or my failure alone," shrugged Filippo. His hands separated a mold with extreme care, revealing half of a golden egg. He breathed a sigh of relief, saying, "Halfway there."

After Filippo removed half of a golden egg from the other mold, Donatello examined one of the halves. "That mold you created actually worked, but do you think this will be enough to show your abilities and impress them?"

"It had better," said Filippo.

"It's constructed very well, but you *are* aware it is a golden egg box?"

"Yes, I know it's a golden egg box."

"Just making sure, because I've never heard of anyone asking for a golden egg box. What do you put in it?"

"Stuff. And what are the other things people are asking for?" demanded Filippo.

"Maestro Umberto mentioned something earlier about a contest to finish the Baptistery's doors."

"You don't say! What are the requirements to enter?"

"A bronze panel depicting something biblical," said Donatello.

"Donatello, your skills of working with bronze are already beyond Maestro Umberto. You should enter, and surely you will win."

"It did cross my mind. However, Maestro Umberto rejected the scene I wished to depict rather quickly, something about upsetting the masses and potentially bringing about Revelations. My intended vision was hung, drawn, and quartered, thus leaving nothing more than dead and jaded memories," recollected Donatello.

Filippo squinted through a magnifying glass as he worked on a hinge connected to a golden egg. "Dead memories for you, but maybe not for me. I might enter that contest, though."

"You should, and not just because your best friend is entering."

"You just said you were *not* entering."

"Not me, your other best friend, Lorenzo Ghiberti," said Donatello.

Filippo crossed his arms in disgust and said, "I hate that guy."

Donatello chuckled, "Really? Since when?"

"How I wish that pompous jackass would get gored by a bull's horn!"

Donatello laughed, "Maybe you'll get lucky, and he'll catch a case of plague and die."

Later that evening, Filippo walked into his house holding a box in his hands. He expected to find his parents, but only his sister, Cassandra, sat at the table peeling vegetables. "Where is everyone?" asked Filippo.

Cassandra answered, "Father caught Modesto altering some of his notes and parchments, one of which was that recent contract with Signore Medici. Needless to say, he was not pleased with our youngest brother. Be careful if you cross paths with him tonight. He's not in a jovial mood."

She noticed the box and asked, "What's in the box?"

"The culmination of my skill and work as a goldsmith," Filippo said.

"Open it. I want to see," urged Cassandra.

Filippo opened the box and removed the golden egg.

"Is that an egg? A golden egg?"

He opened up the egg. "It's a box."

Cassandra examined the egg. "It's quite small. What on earth do you plan on putting in it? Spices? Pebbles?"

Filippo returned the egg back to the box. "It's supposed to show my skill as an artisan."

"Well...I must say it is without any doubt the fanciest golden egg box that I've ever seen."

"Thanks, I think."

Their father's stomping footsteps alerted them to his presence before he entered the room. When Cassandra saw him she averted her gaze. However, Filippo took a step forward with the box in hand. "I have something to show you, Father," he said, revealing the golden egg.

Brunellesco appeared offended. "What is it?"

"It's a mere representation of my talent as a goldsmith," stuttered Filippo.

"You made a gold rock?"

"It's a gold egg. And a box."

"Who in their right mind would spend money on such a frivolous item like a golden egg box? The Pope? When will you finally put your skills to use, Filippo? You keep saying it's only a matter of time and now you show me an egg!"

"I'm entering a contest with the winner getting a contract to finish the Baptistery doors."

Brunellesco smugly stared down Filippo. "You think your talent is worthy of those doors?"

"Oh, I will win. Why would I enter if I thought otherwise even for the briefest of moments?"

"Very well, Filippo. Let's see if your talent can match your words. If you win, you will show me you have found your field. If you do not, you're working for me."

Filippo briefly considered his alternatives. "What if I fail to win, and then I fail to work for you?" he asked brazenly.

Brunellesco looked sternly at his son. "You will not be welcome back into this house."

Filippo stared into his father's eyes and spoke with conviction, "Good thing I'm going to win."

"In time, we'll see," replied Brunellesco, as he turned around and exited the kitchen.

"Oh, Filippo, it looks like your golden egg box might make you homeless," commented Cassandra.

Filippo knew better than to waste finite energy on this trivial game of verbal sparring. Without even making eye contact, he gathered his golden egg box and walked out of the kitchen. High walls adorned in tapestries guided him through the entrance hall and up the marble steps of the front staircase. His hand gripped the cherry wood banister carved to resemble a peregrine falcon. Aside from working overtime, Brunellesco's only hobby was falconry, and he wanted all to know that he had the financial means to pursue such an expensive pastime. However, Filippo was deeply resentful of his father's interests in falconry ever since he had been attacked by one of his father's falcons over a cut of beef. Despite his resentments, Filippo was able to feel a jealous appreciation for the birds and their freedom of flight. As a boy he had watched countless times as birds flew up into the sky, only to become dwindling dots before finally vanishing in the distance.

At the top of the stairs Giuliana surprised Filippo from behind, saying, "Your father told me about the ultimatum he gave you."

"Father wants me to fail. He wants to sacrifice me for his profession. In his eyes, I am no different from Isaac bound atop the stone altar. And he is Abraham wielding a knife at the throat of my dreams. Mother, you have my word, I will find a way to prove him wrong."

"I know you will, my son. But remember, he only wants the best for you."

"The best for me? Or the best for himself?"

Giuliana smiled at her eldest son. "Must those two entities be at war? Perhaps they can coexist? Remember, Filippo, Abraham did place the knife on Isaac's throat, but both were surely laughing and drinking wine that night together."

In the middle of the night Filippo stirred in his sleep, struck by a sudden inspiration. Capitalizing upon creativity's call, he kicked off the sheets and lit a candle from the room's fireplace. With that single candle flame, Filippo lit many other candles, and within seconds, the room blazed bright with candlelight. At his desk, his index finger and thumb held a pencil with extreme care as he drew various images. For hours he concentrated on putting his dreams on paper, until the sun rose through the window in his room. Filippo lifted his head up from the paper and greeted the dawn with a smile. However, the brief distraction allowed him to become aware of the pain in his wrist and arm. He shook out his hand and pored over the countless sheets of paper at his feet before gathering them up. Perusing his drawings, Filippo ripped up the ones he considered unrepresentative of his talent. After careful consideration, Filippo held a single piece of paper up while dozens of other drawings lay in shreds at his feet. He placed it in front of the window and stared at the sunlight bleeding through the paper.

"You will win me the contest," said Filippo, as creativity fluttered away for the time being, leaving him with the physical aches and pains of having worked through the night. He attempted to return to the warm confines of his bed but only got a few steps before he fell to the ground, asleep.

Chapter Five

FLORENCE, 1402

Seven goldsmiths journeyed through the Tuscan lands with their artistic pride leading them into the Baptistery. Each artist stood proudly next to their bronze-plated submissions while silently critiquing the other works. Only Filippo kept his work hidden beneath a burlap shroud, leaving speculation to run rampant in the minds of the other contestants. Having already met or at least heard of the other artists, Filippo knew the various egos competing against him and chose to start the competition early.

The Baptistery's doors swung open, and a loud creak echoed throughout the interior. A middle-aged man stood in the open doorway and eyed the artists. Giovanni di Bicci de' Medici needed no introduction, as everyone in Europe knew of his legendary successes in the financial world. Born to a destitute family, Giovanni had amassed a fortune with his keen intellect and ability to predict the actions of individuals and cities alike.

His two teenage sons, Cosimo and Lorenzo, flanked him. The eldest son, Cosimo de' Medici, had been groomed to be the heir apparent to Giovanni. He had an elongated, slanted nose that many compared to a hawk's beak. Meanwhile, Lorenzo, the younger son, looked just like his father except taller. At an early age Lorenzo had demonstrated a high social aptitude but he lacked any financial skills. Giovanni took note and thus began to have him tutored in multiple languages. Despite both excelling at their chosen fields, the boys were still teenagers and behaved as such. Their presence that morning at the Baptistery was punishment for having talked back to their father with typical teenage insolence. Giovanni decided that waking each of them up early and making them accompany him that morning would make them think twice about being insolent again.

Giovanni turned back to the artists and addressed both of his sons. "If either of you acts up during this, you'll be cleaning chamber pots for a month. Now, repeat what I just said, so I know you understand."

Cosimo gave an affirming nod. "I will not act up."

"And?" continued Giovanni.

"Or I will be cleaning chamber pots for a month," replied Cosimo.

Giovanni stared at his other son. "Your turn, Lorenzo."

Lorenzo sighed. "Unlike my brother, I actually will not act up. But if he does and I get blamed, I'll be cleaning chamber pots for a month."

Giovanni snarled at Lorenzo. "Enough!" he said.

"Yes, Father."

"Which one of you are Leo and Piero?" asked Giovanni, but there was no reply.

Giovanni asked again. "None of you are Leo and Piero?" The artists shook their heads in the negative.

"*Merda*," complained Giovanni. "Guess we have to wait."

Cosimo asked, "Father, who exactly are Leo and Piero?"

"Don't you listen to a damn thing I say, Cosimo?" griped Giovanni. "Lorenzo, please inform your brother who they are."

Lorenzo spoke back stiltingly. "They are, um, two, yes, two names for men. So, both names are male. Leo might belong to a lion or a constellation of a lion."

Giovanni interrupted, saying, "I'm going to cut you off there, Lorenzo, before you further embarrass yourself and our family name. I told both of you earlier, Leo and Piero are the representatives from the Cloth Importers Guild and both will join me in judging the contest today."

"Then where are they?" asked Cosimo.

"If I knew that, I'd send one of you to go retrieve them, but I don't, now do I?" said Giovanni.

Lorenzo badgered Giovanni with a question. "Simply out of curiosity, would you have sent either Cosimo or me? Because I know I would find them."

"Dear brother, the only thing you could find would be failure, because I'm faster than you," Cosimo quipped in reply. "Plus, you get lost in the wine cellar on a weekly basis."

Before Lorenzo could reply, Giovanni spoke. "Either way, it's akin to having chickens or goats pulling a carriage, or maybe one goat and one chicken, after they've been stewed in a pot for a day. Regardless, both of you would surely find a way to mess up. Just sit down, and we'll wait for them to come. I believe it's called the patient game." As he sat down, the Baptistery's doors creaked open. Giovanni said, "Let this be a lesson to all, when the Divine hears my words, my words are delivered."

Leo and Piero staggered into the building visibly intoxicated. "We made it," hiccupped Piero, leaning on the doorframe.

"I'm glad I told you to be here an hour ago," said Giovanni.

"We did. But we ran across him," slurred Leo.

"And who is him?" inquired Giovanni.

A third individual, an upper-class male, made his way between Leo and Piero sipping on a goat bladder of wine, then spoke. "My new friends told me about a bronze plate competition, and because I am the famous and greatly talented artist, Bartolucci di Ghiberti, they could not pass up my opinion."

"Very well. If you can add a judge, then my sons Cosimo and Lorenzo here shall also have a say," declared Giovanni.

Leo shrugged, saying, "I have no objections."

Bartolucci interjected. "But what do two teenage *marmocchi* know about judging bronze work?"

A stern Giovanni glared at Bartolucci, but Piero intervened. "It's quite all right. Do you think Leo or I know what we're doing? Let's just get this started already."

The six judges began judging on the opposite side of Filippo. Bartolucci stepped in front of the others and praised the work of the first artist, saying, "It's magnificent! A talent worthy to represent Florence on such a sacred building."

Giovanni elbowed Bartolucci out of the way to examine the bronze panel displaying the sacrifice of Isaac by Abraham. In a grand display of elegance, Abraham calmly aimed the point of a knife at an equally relaxed Isaac. In the sky an angel hovered over Isaac with an outstretched hand reaching to stop Abraham. Subtle details like curls in the hair and creases in the fabric had been meticulously crafted in what appeared to be a relatively peaceful scene.

"It is a superb demonstration of skill," said Giovanni, then asked the first artist, "What is your name?"

"Lorenzo."

Giovanni smiled, "Wonderful. Just like my son. Now, what is your surname?"

Lorenzo sheepishly answered, "Ghiberti."

Giovanni raised his eyebrow with curiosity, "Ghiberti, huh? Are you related to the new judge? He, too, is a talented metal worker."

Leo spoke up. "Didn't you say that was your son, Bartolucci? Like when we were walking here?"

Bartolucci feigned surprise. "Lorenzo? Is that really you, my son? I didn't recognize you against the blinding beauty of your work."

Giovanni spoke softly to his sons, "A blind mute could see who will receive his vote. I'm glad I dragged you two along. Remember, stay quiet and let me talk."

The judges gathered around the second artist, Jacopo della Querra. Leo stared in confusion at the panel and asked, "Did he even *do* anything?"

Stepping in front of Leo, Piero investigated for himself and said, "Let me look." And he did, but even Piero walked away scratching his head.

"What biblical scene is this supposed to be?" asked Giovanni.

Jacopo cleared his throat. "It is the great deluge that spared only Noah, but this is depicted from the perspective of a fish."

"Clever, but you didn't really do anything artistic," said Giovanni. "Next!"

More of an enthusiastic hobbyist than a professional gold-smith, Simona da Colla's work demonstrated his limited talent in metalworking. However, the chosen subject matter boggled the minds of the judges.

Leo's mouth gaped open. "Is that really what I think it is?"

The primary figure on the bronze plate was a donkey sitting on a stool scratching its chin with a hoof, as humans surrounding him ask questions. Despite the absurdity of the scene, the work showed skill.

"Yes, it's a talking donkey," clarified Simona. "If you remember in the book of Numbers, Book 22, they have a donkey that talks. And as I was told, we had to present a scene from the Old Testament. Is Numbers no longer in the Old Testament? Or did I fail to receive the correspondence about the change?"

Leo and Piero shrugged before looking at Giovanni, who said, "Let's ask our new judges for their opinion."

"I agree," concurred Bartolucci. "What are your thoughts, Cosimo and Lorenzo?"

"I guess it's a very nicely done talking donkey," surmised Cosimo.

Lorenzo asked Simona, "What other scenes do you see yourself depicting, if you win the contract?"

"Other scenes?" The question baffled Simona. "I was thinking of putting a giant talking donkey on the door. What about that?"

"Somehow, I can't see the city of Florence being represented by a giant talking donkey," Giovanni stated, before he turned his back to move on to the next artist.

The oldest goldsmith vying for the door contract, Niccolo d'Arezzo had honed his craft over decades by plying his trade between Florence and Venice. When Filippo heard of his entry, he knew the savvy artist would provide fierce competition. And upon seeing Niccolo's bronze plate Filippo knew that he was right to worry. Niccolo's work depicted Moses parting the Red Sea: towering waves extended upward to the heavens, dwarfing the fleeing Israelites below.

"Quite a work, but I want to see less landscape and more Moses," critiqued Bartolucci.

"I actually reached the same conclusion," said Giovanni.

The next artist, Francesco di Valdambrino, turned his entry around before the judges could get a good look at it. "I withdraw mine to avoid embarrassment."

"Really?" asked Giovanni.

"I feel my work does not live up to the standards set by these other artists."

"Very well then," said Giovanni. "Next!"

The sixth artist, Volfango, dabbled in goldsmithing but rat catching remained his true passion, especially after having developed a taste for directly ingesting rat poison. However, what he did not know was that the mercury and lead in the poison left him senile, which was reflected in his art.

"What's that jagged line?" asked Leo.

"Are you an *idiota*?!" screamed Volfagno. "It's clearly a snake!"

"It is?" asked Piero.

Volfango yelled back, saying, "You are blinder than Isaac!" His insults echoed through the vast open room.

"Next," declared Giovanni.

The judges gathered around the last artist, Filippo, and his covered plate. Motioning to Filippo to unveil his work, Giovanni commented, "I don't even know what it is, but by keeping it hidden, you have had me wanting to know since I walked in today."

Filippo removed the cloth to reveal his work. A collective gasp escaped everyone's lips upon seeing his depiction of the Sacrifice of Isaac. Filippo's bronze panel captured the raw, emotional torment visibly tearing Abraham up as he seizes a bound Isaac by the throat and places the knife to his son's throat. An angel clutches the forearm of Abraham's knife-wielding hand and appears to struggle to keep the blade away from Isaac's throat.

Giovanni looked at the panel, awe-struck, then spoke, "Remarkable. And as a father, I, too, know how he feels, almost every waking moment."

"One can see the entire story from this one panel," gasped Leo.

Piero agreed, "The emotion leaps out."

"It's mediocre. Not great, but a decent, average attempt nonetheless," said Bartolucci, brushing off Filippo's work. "As a judge, Lorenzo receives my vote."

"Of course he does. If you voted against him, it would be awkward at the dinner table," rebuked Giovanni. "My vote goes to Filippo here."

Piero studied all the entries one last time. After a moment, he reached his decision, saying, "I'm going with the Talking Donkey."

Giovanni looked toward his sons. "Cosimo, Lorenzo, whom do you choose?" he asked.

While they contemplated their answer, Bartolucci secretly removed a bag of gold and placed it in Leo's hand. Leo opened the bag wide enough to see the glint of gold, then said, "I vote for Lorenzo."

Giovanni told his sons, "You two have the last remaining votes. Please choose wisely, for your choice will determine which artist's dreams come true today. And remember who brought you here and whose roof you sleep under too."

Without hesitation, Cosimo spoke up. "Filippo," he said.

"A part of me is leaning toward the Talking Donkey, but there's something about Volfango's anger I find amusing. He gets my vote," said Lorenzo.

Giovanni crossed his arms, annoyed. "Is that your choice, son?"

"Yes, Father, because I wanted to sleep in this morning," retorted Lorenzo.

After counting the votes in his head, Leo announced, "It's a tie."

"Then both Lorenzo Ghiberti and Filippo Brunelleschi will receive the commission," declared Giovanni.

"What?" fumed Filippo.

Leo agreed. "That sounds like a fair and balanced compromise to me," he said.

Even Bartolucci reluctantly complied. "My son Lorenzo and Filippo can split the work, and each can do half."

But Filippo was very angry. Through gritted teeth, he said, "I will not work with that arrogant hack. First of all, he tried to rig the competition with his father. But more importantly, his style embodies everything that disgusts me about art. Look at his work. I ask every father in here: If you had to kill your son, would you do so while looking like you were deciding on which whore to pick in a brothel? And for every son, look at Ghiberti's Isaac. If your father held a knife to your throat, would you be calmer than the seas outside Ostia?"

Filippo reached for a sculpting blade and pointed it at Ghiberti, who cowered in fear. Keeping his eyes locked on a nervous Ghiberti, Filippo addressed all in attendance. "See, this is what fear looks like, as he wonders which breath will be his final one. Does he even remotely resemble that atrocity in bronze you see there?"

Bartolucci attempted to intervene between the two artists, but Filippo turned the blade at him and said, "Your nepotism defiles not just this House of God and the integrity of this competition, but you desecrate all of Florence."

"And Filippo, it is your ire that prevents you from going any further in this contest," said Giovanni. "Because of your unexpected outburst, Lorenzo Ghiberti is awarded the contract to finish the Baptistery's doors."

Filippo dropped the sculpting blade on the floor, pleading to Giovanni, "No, I can't lose!"

"But you did," said Bartolucci nastily. "Come, Lorenzo, let's go celebrate your win."

As everyone left the Baptistery, Filippo stared up, almost as if watching his dreams float away. Giovanni motioned for his sons to leave the building, then appeared behind Filippo, patting him on the back, and said, "You have talent and ability, young man. But today, you beat yourself. Sometimes one's worst enemy is that son of a *cagna* staring back in the mirror."

Filippo dropped his gaze to the polished marble floor and looked at his reflection. "I only wanted to demonstrate that Ghiberti's work doesn't represent real life. We are creatures filled with emotion, and that emotion needs to be captured."

"Perhaps you could have thought of a better way to show that, instead of attempted murder," Giovanni reminded him. "But don't let this experience deter you from your dreams. Though I may not have bested every trial and tribulation life placed before me, there were lessons to be learned simply from the experience alone. My first experience with banking was beyond disastrous. Some tricksters promised me great riches if I made a small investment in their company."

"What was the company?" asked Filippo.

"Please don't laugh. But magical grape seeds capable of growing in any climate. Needless to say, my youthful aspirations of wealth guided my financial folly. Eventually, I realized I had been tricked. When I tracked down the *stronzi*, there were more of them than myself. They did get the better of me, but I was able to hit the one who sold me the seeds so hard in the jaw that he still cannot enjoy solid foods to this day. My knuckle never did fully heal right. Look for yourself."

Giovanni displayed his deformed knuckles and said, "Each morning, I remember getting swindled. That single experience has helped deter countless similar situations from happening, all from this little reminder."

Filippo stared at Giovanni earnestly and said, "Trust me, my failings on this day have been forever seared into my memory."

Chapter Six

FLORENCE, 1402

After leaving the Baptistery earlier that morning, Filippo joined Donatello at a tavern, *L'Ubriaco Felice*. The darkness provided a safe refuge for Filippo, and the flow of libations helped dull his memory of defeat. Across from him Donatello hurried to finish the contents of a wooden goblet, then turned to the bartender and said, "Another bottle, please." He smiled at Filippo. "Not only are you a worthy goldsmith, but you are proving yourself a worthy drinking partner."

"He cheated his way into the contract," pouted Filippo.

The bartender arrived with their next round and asked, "May I add this to your bill of sale?"

"Oh, definitely not," stated Donatello. "However, my father, Niccolo di Betto Bardi, comes in here all the time. Add this to his account."

The bartender asked, "You mean the Wool Merchants' Guild's account?"

"That's the one," responded Donatello. "Put everything we've had today on it."

"I hope you two realize that it's no longer day," said the bartender, walking away.

"How long have we been here?" asked Filippo.

Donatello took a long sip and said, "Not long enough, so drink up. Back to the competition: even by your account, you threatened to kill Lorenzo."

"Kill? Not kill per se," explained Filippo, slurring his words. "Maybe slash or slightly maim, but it was primarily intended to show an example of the proper emotional response. But I admit I can see where I may have alarmed some." He set his mug down, then said, "Is it already night?"

Donatello pointed to a patron leaving the bar. When pushing the door open, the night sky filled the top of the doorframe for a brief second. Standing up from the table, Filippo told Donatello, "I must leave," then staggered to the door and off into the Florentine night.

When Filippo entered his house, the alcohol in his system forced him to rely on reflex and instinct. His drunkenness also blurred his memory of the events of the day. After closing the door, a voice called out from the darkness. "And? How did you do?" asked Giuliana.

Full of remorse, Filippo remembered his outburst at the Baptistery and his subsequent failure so he answered her question with his head hung in shame. While he reflected on his actions, Brunellesco appeared from behind and gave him a comforting pat on the back. Before he spoke, Brunellesco gauged Filippo's mood and held his tongue.

Finally, Filippo opened his eyes and said, "I gave my word, and now I shall honor it."

He hurried up the stairs, down the hall, and into his room. He grabbed a handful of clothes and wrapped them in a bundle on his bed. But then a distant memory crossed his thoughts. He lifted up his mattress to reveal a pouch of gold coins.

"You don't have to do this, Filippo," said Brunellesco from the doorway to the room.

Filippo finished packing his bundle of clothes and said, "I don't want to be a notary."

"Where will you go?" asked Brunellesco.

"Somewhere other than here."

Brunellesco sniffed theatrically, then said, "You're drunk and not thinking clearly. You'll be back by tomorrow evening."

Walking by his father, Filippo said, "And when I'm not?"

He bounded down the stairs with fervent resolve. Lingering in the entrance hall, Giuliana spotted Filippo walking to the door and asked him, "Where are you going at this late hour? You just got back."

Filippo opened the door and answered her. "I'm leaving," he said decisively.

"Is this about that stupid bet you and your father had?"

"His life belongs to him, not me, and I'd much rather learn to live my own."

Brunellesco sauntered down the stairs and said, "Let him leave and sleep on the street like a stray dog. He'll be back when he sobers up in the morning."

Guiliana pleaded with Filippo, saying, "Your father doesn't mean that."

But it was too late. Filippo stepped outside and closed the door behind him.

Soon he found himself outside the southern gates of Florence, staring above at the countless stars lighting up the night sky and wondered, "Which way do I go from here?"

"Filippo! Wait!" called out Donatello, running through the gates behind him.

Filippo stopped as Donatello caught up with him and said, panting, "You're not the only one leaving this damn city!"

The starlight revealed bloodstains on Donatello's tunic. "Who does that blood belong to?" asked Filippo.

"Some of it is mine. Actually, probably, most of it is mine," answered Donatello.

Filippo gestured toward the wound. "Who did you hit?"

"Oh, I didn't just hit him. My fist nearly bludgeoned his damned brains," beamed Donatello.

"Then who now has bludgeoned brains?"

"My father said he was going to kill me for that bar tab earlier. He tried, but my fist was able to succeed. Now, we need to put distance between Florence and us before he wakes up. I don't know if I could do it again. Pretty sure it's broken."

As they walked away from Florence, Filippo turned to Donatello. "Where should we go?"

"Anywhere but Florence."

"Right now we're traveling south."

"Anything in the south?"

Filippo thought for a moment, then responded, "Rome."

"Have you ever been?"

"No."

"Neither have I. How will we know the way to get there?"

"Don't they say all roads lead to Rome?"

"Except for the ones leading away from Rome. Now, drink up," said Donatello as he handed Filippo a bladder of wine.

Beneath a calm night sky, the two friends staggered south with Florence to their backs.

Chapter Seven

APPIAN WAY, 1402

Filippo struggled to open his eyes. Each time his eyelids parted, the painfully bright sunlight forced them back shut. Almost at the point of tears, he called for help, but a rasp escaped his dehydrated mouth. His eyes adjusted, assisted by momentary clouds that briefly blocked out the searing light. He squinted his eyes shut again, only to fall off the back of a cart that he could not remember ever getting on.

On the well-worn stone path Filippo writhed in severe pain, then he heard Donatello's voice saying, "I don't think he's dead. He's moving somewhat. Hey, Filippo, are you dead?"

Filippo responded with a slight tilt of his head.

"You're lucky. Do you need help up?" asked Donatello.

Filippo moved his head up and down only a fraction in either direction.

"Hold on," said Donatello, as he hopped out from the front of the cart. Helping Filippo up to his feet, he asked him, "Did that hurt? It sounded like it did."

Filippo pointed to his throat. Unable to speak in whole words, his vocal chords scraped out only syllables. "Wa-wa-wa," he said.

Donatello laughed. "Water? Why would we need water when we have breakfast wine?" He handed Filippo a bladder of wine and spoke, "We have a saying in my family. To avoid a hangover, drink plenty of breakfast wine."

Squeezing the bladder overhead, Filippo guzzled the wine, spilling some in the process. Without hesitation, Donatello grabbed the bladder to prevent more from spilling. "I accidentally drank the lunch wine and the dinner wine, so that is all we have left until tonight."

Hydrated and satiated but still in pain, Filippo screamed, startling Donatello. "I could not scream when my skull shattered on the ground. My throat was too parched, so that was for that," explained Filippo.

"No need for that. It sounded pretty painful and unpleasant," assured Donatello.

"Oh, there's one more thing. What happened last night, and where are we?" asked Filippo.

"You don't remember?"

"If I did, would I be asking you?"

"In that case, you lost to Lorenzo to get the commission for the Baptistery's doors."

Filippo remembered. "Damn it. Why did you bring that up?"

"Because you asked. After consoling your loss on the tab of my father's guild, you told your father off, slapped your mother, punted your little brother off a bridge, or something along those lines. Whatever happened, you decided to leave. And now we're going to Rome. At some point, we met Miriam up there, and she was kind enough to give us a ride there." Donatello pointed to the front of the cart at Miriam, a bovine woman who was holding the reins.

Regret and remorse flooded through Filippo. Ashamed, he asked, "What did I do? I must go back."

Donatello pulled him back and asked, "What would you do back in Florence? Work for your father? Or maybe apprentice under Lorenzo?"

Miriam interrupted. "And we're over halfway there."

"Did you hear Miriam? We're almost in Rome," said Donatello.

After a brief deliberation, he responded, "Did I bring anything with me at least?"

Donatello pointed to a bundle on the cart and told Filippo, "You brought whatever is in there."

Later that evening, Miriam directed the cows to a quaint inn nestled off the paved road. "If we're to make it to Rome, we'll need to let the cattle rest and feed for the night," she said.

"Which means we can restock our wine supply," said Donatello.

"You have not lived until you sip the aqua vitae served here," said Miriam.

Upon entering the inn, Miriam waved to the barkeep. "Three of your most potent elixirs to cure us of our sobriety."

Filippo looked at the intoxicated patrons at the inn, but the sight conjured up memories of last night's mistakes.

"Come, let us find a place to sit amongst our fellow travelers," said Donatello as he led the way into the raucous crowd.

Moments later, the barkeep appeared with three mugs sloshing frothy liquid over the rims. Filippo stared at the mug before him on a table. All the mistakes he had made the time last he had been drunk rushed into his mind, and he pushed the drink away.

"Not thirsty?" inquired Donatello.

"The damage was done last night, my friend," explained Filippo. "I need to get some fresh air. If you need me, I'll be outside."

Donatello waved to Filippo, then turned his attention to Miriam.

Outside it was a brisk night; two massive Roman aqueducts rose from the ground before stretching off into the distance, and the sight proved to be a muse for Filippo. Inspired, he rushed to his bundle on the back of Miriam's cart and removed a sheet of parchment and charcoal. His hand directed the charcoal all over the paper's surface as he drew the two aqueducts vanishing over the horizon.

Filippo experienced déjà vu when he woke up in the harsh sunlight and watched the Italian countryside drift past him. He saw Miriam in front cracking the reins and Donatello at her side rummaging through his drawings.

Donatello turned around to say, "I never knew you could draw this well. These are very well drawn."

Filippo wiped his eyes, yawning, and replied, "I've been experimenting with a more realistic style. Notice how the aqueducts vanish over the horizon at the same point."

Miriam leaned over Donatello's shoulder to look at the pictures. "It's like your drawing leaps off the paper."

Donatello added, "Or you could leap into the paper."

Examining his surroundings, Filippo noticed a massive wall behind them and asked, "Speaking of horizons, what city is that behind us?"

"Oh, that? That's Rome. Miriam said it's not all it used to be," answered Donatello.

"That's Rome? Then where are we going?"

"To Miriam's family's pig farm."

"A pig farm? I don't want to go to a pig farm," exclaimed Filippo. "No offense to you, Miriam. I'm sure it's a lovely place and all, but the legendary stories of Rome have fascinated me for as long as I can remember."

Donatello grasped for straws. "Well, it's not just a pig farm. They have chickens, sheep, and a goat named Clompy. And cows. Did you have cows or Clompy the goat in Florence?"

"Well, the cows are currently with us," said Miriam.

"Okay, so the farm is currently lacking cows."

Filippo crossed his arms and said, "You know what else it lacks?"

Donatello fell for the bait, asking, "What?"

"Taverns," replied Filippo. With that, he reached up and grabbed his drawings from Donatello's hands, then hopped off the cart and walked back in the direction of Rome.

Donatello stared at Miriam with soulful eyes. "He presents a very persuasive argument."

"And remember, where there are taverns, there are women," yelled Filippo.

"Life is pulling us in opposite directions. Where our love was once as sturdy as an oak, destiny has decided to split us apart as if with an ax. I must go, my dear," said Donatello. He kissed Miriam on the cheek, then jumped off the cart, running to catch up with Filippo.

Donatello slowed down when he neared Filippo and said, "So, where are these taverns and women of which you spoke?"

"See those walls?"

Donatello nodded.

"Inside, my friend."

"Then what are we waiting for?" asked Donatello before sprinting off toward Rome.

Moments later, Filippo caught up to Donatello, who was out of breath and covered in sweat. Donatello lifted his head up for a deep breath and said, "It looks so much closer than it really is."

The two friends approached Rome at a leisurely pace on the Appian Way. Beneath the soles of their feet were stones that had been laid down in 312 BC under orders of the Roman censor Appius Claudius Caecus. Originally intended as a military road connecting Italy's southeast coast for Roman soldiers to quell riots in Brindisi, the road would soon take on a commercial purpose allowing for trade from all over. Because of the vast numbers of people traveling the Appian Way, those in charge quickly realized its potential as a political tool. When Spartacus led his rebellion against Rome in 73 BC, Roman forces ended the uprising within two years. Some six thousand slaves would be used to convey a political message, as they were all crucified along the Appian Way. The macabre sight ensured that Rome would win against any rebellion, whether mounted by slaves or citizens.

Although the bodies of Roman dissenters had long since decayed, other means of propaganda still existed. Massive mausoleums decorated the roadsides, each more ornate the closer they were to Rome. Filippo stopped in the shadow of one gargantuan tomb that was carved from marble. Although dilapidated, its former glory was evident. Filippo read an inscription out loud: "Here rests the family of Lucius Aelius Cassius, Commander of the Eleventh Legion."

"When our lives are over and we rot in the ground, do you think those after us will even remember us?" asked Donatello.

Filippo pondered the question briefly, then said, "If they are to write about us centuries from now, they surely won't be writing about our exploits in front of an abandoned structure dedicated to the dead. Perhaps that's why we're walking through their graveyard; it is to remind us of how precious life is and how all our time is finite. Eventually, we will all be like Lucius here. And hopefully, they will still be talking about us."

Chapter Eight

ROME, 1402

Outside Rome Filippo and Donatello journeyed up the Via Appia north toward the massive structure known as the Aurelian Walls. Following the Pax Romana, where peace stretched throughout the Empire as far as Roman roads, an invasion of Germanic tribes known as the Vandals brought an abrupt end to Rome's stability in the third century. The Roman Emperor Aurelian commissioned the Aurelian Walls to enlarge the existing Servian Wall in an effort to fortify Rome's defense in case of another barbarian onslaught. When construction finished in the year 275 AD, concrete blocks formed massive walls fifty feet high and twenty-five feet thick that stretched for twelve miles and encircled an area of five square miles. Three hundred and eighty towers, each paced a hundred feet apart, provided constant security to ensure Rome's continued existence.

Donatello craned his head up to look at the top of the Aurelian Walls and said, "Thankfully, the gate's open. I don't know if I'd be able to push you over the wall without the aid of a catapult."

"Today, I'd rather not try and fly, then surely die," joked Filippo. "I still can't believe I'm going through with this."

"You mean *us*."

"Donatello, didn't you want to go play farmer? Pretty sure you did."

"I wanted to meet Clompy the goat, but alas, I did not. And now I'm here with you to conquer Rome and its taverns and brothels."

The two friends laughed as they entered Rome through the southeast gate, the Porta Appia, surrounded by two circular stone towers rising out of the wall. Passing beneath the stone arch, Donatello asked, "Well, we're finally here. What should we do first?"

Without hesitation, Filippo replied, "I already know."

"And?" wondered Donatello.

A youthful exuberance radiated out from Filippo as he talked. "Ever since I can remember, my parents told me stories of the Coliseum's grandeur."

"Can't be that grand, if I've never heard of it," answered Donatello.

Filippo closed his eyes. "Imagine thousands of eyes watching two brave gladiators fight on the Coliseum's floor."

Donatello chuckled and said, "Growing up at my house, one could always find a fight happening on the floor."

"Supposedly, there were times they rerouted the aqueducts to flood the Coliseum for naval times."

The words captivated Donatello. "From what you're saying, I should expect to see some fights and some boat battles. My hopes better not be dashed."

Filippo shrugged. "Your guess is as good as mine. I have only been there in my imagination. But you know the Roman Empire no longer exists, right?"

The question stupefied Donatello. "So, where are we, if Rome no longer exists?"

Beneath an amethyst sky, Filippo and Donatello sauntered up a hill with a sense of increasing satisfaction in their steps. At the top of the hill amidst dilapidated buildings, they spotted the massive columns supporting the aqueduct known as the Aqua Claudia. They journeyed north on the road and eventually beheld the Coliseum from a distance outlined beneath one of the many stone arches.

Although construction officially began in 72 AD under Emperor Vespasian, the origins of the Flavian Amphitheater or Coliseum can be traced back nearly a decade before to 64 AD. As a great fire razed most of central Rome, the infamous Emperor Nero supposedly watched the chaos while strumming his lyre. When the flames died down, Nero laid claim to the three hundred acres of burned land and built a massive palace, an ostentatious estate only a Roman emperor could devise. Lush landscaped gardens surrounded some three hundred rooms for the emperor's private use, which included an artificial lake known as the Domus Aurea. Nero's "Great House" quickly made all other Romans green with envy because it was emblematic of a luxurious decadence accessible to only one man. In a vain attempt to copy one of the Seven Wonders of the World, Nero commissioned a statue of himself as the Colossus of Rhodes, which stood over ninety feet in height. Four years later in 68 AD, Nero's tyrannical ways and lack of humility cost him dearly. With all of Rome loathing him, he avoided facing public consequences for his actions by instructing his personal secretary to take his life.

In an effort to help eradicate the memory of Nero and smooth over any wounds and resentment among the Roman populace, Vespasian specifically chose the area near the Coliseum. Instead of taxing Roman citizens and leaving them with the costly burden of construction, Vespasian's recent Roman victories in Judah helped finance the eighty-thousand-seat amphitheater. For almost a decade, slaves transported massive stones nearly twenty miles from the city of Tivolo to Rome, where artisans sculpted statues of gods and goddesses to adorn alcoves. Unfortunately, Vespasian never lived to see his architectural tribute to Rome, dying in 79 AD. His son and successor, Emperor Titus, saw the structure fully finished and presided over the inaugural games held within it around 81 AD.

Within no time, institutionalized slaughter became synonymous with the Coliseum. Rome believed that its people suffered from furor, an irrational emotion, which the games helped suppress by allowing those in attendance to live vicariously through the violence and carnage. The Roman Senate and those wielding powers knew that keeping the general populace subdued would prevent any potential uprisings and subsequent destruction. When Roman citizens found the games becoming rather dull, certain proactive measures were put in place to amp up the spectacle. The number of people on the Coliseum floor would be increased to allow for the reenactment of actual battles from Roman history that would exemplify imperial might. However, by the time Filippo and Donatello gazed upon the Coliseum, those days of glory were far in the past. All that remained was the ruined stone carcass of a long-forgotten architectural leviathan.

Donatello appeared less than impressed and asked, "This is it? I mean, yes, it's big, but it's like looking at the picked bones of a turkey after a big feast you were not invited to."

As they walked beneath one of the many arched entrances, a strong smell overwhelmed them. Filippo pinched his nose shut and asked, "Did something die nearby? What is that vile stench?"

"Many, many somethings must have died all around us to produce a smell so rotten and vile," replied Donatello.

Filippo shook his head in disgust, then waved for Donatello to follow him farther into the ruins. Walking out into the open center, Filippo swung an imaginary sword as if fighting invisible opponents. Between sword strikes, he said, "Imagine the thunderous roar of the crowd. All their senses focused upon you and your enemy, as you battle to the death!"

"Are those sword skills? Or are you a fool struggling to keep his head afloat and not drown?" remarked Donatello caustically. "Can we leave now?"

"Why would you want to go anywhere else?" asked Filippo.

"Well, for one, ever since the last gladiators left, it appears all of Rome turned this into a combination of a trash heap and public chamber pot."

In the distance atop one of the higher levels, Filippo spotted a few other people. "We're not the only ones here. See, there are others," he said.

Donatello turned to see people removing bricks and dropping them down below. "They're only here to steal building materials. Now let's go before the smell seeps into my clothes permanently and not even tavern girls will talk to me for all the gold in the city."

Donatello drudged through the muddy ground searching for a way out of the Coliseum. Filippo relented when he registered a terrible stench that almost made him gag. He ran to catch up with Donatello, who turned around in relief and said, "Finally, you have come to your senses. Because *my* senses seriously cannot take that any more. I was debating about searing my nose shut to keep that horrendous smell from rotting my brain. The way I look at it, you picked the first thing we did, which was about as much fun as the plague. Now, it's up to me to redeem our Roman adventure with my choice for our next stop."

"And where might that be?" inquired Filippo.

Donatello grinned and said, "Let us be modern gladiators and use our livers to wage war against those various, evil libations within the battlegrounds of a tavern. Or just any place with wine."

Chapter Nine

Since departing the Coliseum earlier that day, Donatello searched for an ideal drinking establishment by aimlessly wandering through the twisting and turning roads of Rome. Filippo struggled to keep up, constantly distracted by the ancient architecture that captured his attention every few steps. Back in Florence, Filippo surely would have grabbed Donatello and insisted that he choose a tavern, but the allure of Rome was impossible for Filippo to resist.

When the sun began to descend beneath the horizon, Donatello stopped abruptly in the road. Entranced by the surrounding buildings, Filippo bumped into Donatello by accident. Filippo apologized, "I'm sorry, my friend. I was too busy looking at the heavens around us."

Donatello paid little attention to the apology, occupied as he was with assessing a tavern nestled on the banks of the Tiber. After a moment, he announced his decision out loud. "There it is," he said.

"Have you finally decided on a tavern?" asked Filippo.

Donatello replied enthusiastically. "It is not just a tavern. The hopes and dreams of patrons fill the air with delightful conversation. It is where the glorious nectar of the gods flows as freely as our ability to choose where to partake of a drink. Such a place contains the power to turn a bad day into a good one by making you forget any and all woes. It holds the power to a happy life within its walls through friendship, food, and fire on a cold night. And don't forget, it allows the common man the chance to procure a small profit through games of fortune."

"I find more flaws in your words than the grapes on all the vines in all the vineyards of Tuscany combined," remarked Filippo, as they walked toward the bar.

Donatello replied, "If you're so critical, I invite you to please deconstruct my praise. And let me remind you, you made me visit a stone chamber pot earlier."

Filippo said, "First, the nectar of the gods is ambrosia."

"Really?" argued Donatello. "It's wine. Everyone knows in wine there is life. Clearly, someone has not read the Bible. And because we're in Rome, let's go track down a priest, a bishop, a cardinal, or even the Pope, so that you can ask him yourself."

"You know that is not what I meant," said Filippo, as he moved on with his next criticism: "Then you are aware wine does not flow freely, or how else would taverns make a profit?"

Donatello dwelled on the question, then said, "I'm sure someone pays at some level or perhaps the Wool Merchants' Guild pays the bill. But if you don't have to pay for it, then the wine technically does flow free."

As Filippo's mind prepared another argument, Donatello intervened and stated, "Enough with bashing my choice. Let's let fate decide if I chose the proper tavern."

Inside the bar, the two friends stood in a poorly lit room with a lone patron drinking from a bottle of wine. Filippo congratulated Donatello with a pat on the back. "All that delightful conversation appears to have been replaced with dreary despair."

"Oh, be quiet," objected Donatello. "It's eccentrically vintage and probably dates back to before ancient Rome, where people considered candles fire demon-ghosts. Hence, the darkness."

Donatello motioned to the barkeep, a rough-looking man with a face that resembled weather-beaten leather, and asked, "One bottle of your finest but cheapest wine."

The decrepit barkeep walked toward them with a wine bottle partially caked in mud. He smiled and opened a mouth that was missing several teeth. He inserted the cork into his mouth, bit down on it with a single tooth, and yanked the bottle away. The cork popped out of the bottle, as did the barkeep's tooth. The barkeep picked the tooth up off the dirty ground and tried to reinsert it back into his gum.

"Care for any wine, Filippo?" offered Donatello.

"I'm well for the moment," said Filippo.

Donatello shrugged and drank straight from the bottle. Mid-sip, he swished the wine around in his mouth, then swallowed it and spat something out onto the tabletop.

Filippo scrutinized the item. "That's a tooth," he pronounced sagely.

Donatello held it up to the light. "Looks like it. At least we know how it got there. Mystery solved." Without hesitation, he took another sip.

"How long did you spend deciding on this place?" asked Filippo

"I'll be honest; I got somewhat lost. But we did end up in a bar nonetheless, so I deserve some credit."

"A bar about to pass into the next life from the look of it."

Donatello held his finger up in pride. "At least it's not making me gag from rotten smells."

Filippo raised his hands in utter disbelief. "You're drinking tooth wine."

Donatello shrugged it off. "It's probably a Roman thing for luck."

"It's not a Roman thing," contended Filippo.

Donatello refused to believe otherwise. "Let me check," he said. He held the bottle up, gulped down the remaining contents, and rose from his chair, emitting a deafening burp. With the wine rushing through his veins, he walked erratically to the only other patron present, a short, chubby, bald man with his back turned. Donatello tried to pat him on the shoulder, but lost his balance and fell forward into him, sending them both crashing to the ground.

"You fool!" screamed the man, as he pushed Donatello off him.

Donatello bowed his head deeply and apologized, "Sorry, my friend, the wine misguided my steps."

"I'm not your friend," contended the man.

Donatello pouted. "You're not my friend? But, my friend, I said I was sorry, my friend."

The man flared his nostrils, then spoke through clenched teeth, "Did you not hear me? Don't call me your friend, for I am not your friend!"

Giggles escaped from Donatello's mouth before he forced it shut.

"Why are you laughing?" demanded the man.

With a slight grin, Donatello explained, "If you must know, when you get mad, a vein atop that desolate mountain you call a head pulses in a humorous fashion, my friend."

The same two words infuriated the man. "I am not your friend. Some call me Bardo the Brazen. Others run away in fear screaming my name: Bardo the Bad."

Donatello interjected, "Surprised no one has called you Bardo the *Bald*. It just seems somewhat fitting with your hairstyle, or lack of one. But I digress." He motioned for the bartender. "Two more bottles of your tooth wine. But this time, less mud on the bottle. Something that you've kept off the ground."

The bartender nodded. Donatello turned back to Bardo and asked, "Do you like drinking, my friend? Of course you do, my friend. Why else would you be here if you did not, my friend? Definitely not for the delightful ambience in this crypt, my friend."

The bartender brought them two bottles of wine. Donatello opened his purse, pulled out two coins, and paid for the wine. "Thank you." As the bartender placed a bottle in his mouth, Donatello waved him off, saying, "You should be saving what teeth you have left. If it's not down to a single tooth by now."

After seeing the gold, Bardo's demeanor changed in an instant. His sullen mood lifted and he beamed a smile. His arms stretched out wide and embraced Donatello like a long-lost friend from childhood. "*Mio amico!*" exclaimed Bardo, still in a haunting baritone deeper than a chasm.

"Like I always say, everyone likes free wine!" rejoiced Donatello.

The new friends toasted their bottles to their newly formed friendship, when Bardo asked him, "What brings you to Roma on such a delightful night?"

"Well, I actually am here with my fellow artist, Filippo," replied Donatello. He turned to Filippo and yelled across the bar, "Hey, I've made a friend. Come say hello."

Filippo left the confines of his well-lit table and walked over to Donatello. Bardo stood up to greet Filippo with even more enthusiasm than before by lifting him off the ground, nearly toppling over himself. "You can set me down now," protested Filippo. Bardo dropped Filippo to the floor, then pulled him up to his feet.

Bardo asked, "With those accents, have either of you ever left Florence before?"

Filippo replied, "No. But I have traveled all over through books."

The answer made Bardo smile even more. "Well, it just so happens I am the man you need to know in Rome."

Filippo scanned Bardo up and down, still unsure. "I doubt that," he said, then he turned to Donatello. "Don't you find it rather unusual he loathed you until you bought him wine?" he asked.

Donatello laughed. "Wine can turn the worst of enemies into the best of friends."

"It's true," added Bardo. "I once saw some wolves and some deer drink a lot of wine and then have a party."

"See, Filippo. There's evidence of such an instance, right there," chided Donatello.

Bardo revealed a set of playing cards in his hands and asked, "Do you any of you partake in fun games of innocence, perhaps with monetary incentives?"

Donatello turned to Filippo and asked, "Hey, can I borrow some money?"

Filippo took a step away. "Don't you have your own to lose?" he asked tartly.

"Oh, I forgot," remembered Donatello, who then placed his coin purse on the table. He cracked his knuckles and smiled at

Bardo. "Like in life, we must accept the cards we are dealt. I will apologize now for taking your money, friend."

Bardo slapped his knee and burst out laughing. "That's a good one! I will remember that when you are penniless."

"Me, penniless? You must have drunkenly confused me for yourself," countered Donatello.

"While you two sit here exchanging laurels of hemlock, I am going to investigate more of this great city," said Filippo, as he turned around for the door.

Bardo cut the cards and asked, "Does he not like money?"

Donatello made sure that Filippo had gone before he said, "We all have our vices. Mine, for instance, are gambling, drinking, and womanizing, in no particular order, though drinking does make the other two more fun. But all are ephemeral, and fun is always fleeting. Filippo is different. His vice is unobtainable. What he seeks is the past."

As he dealt the cards, Bardo understood. "Each man has his own guide to lead him to his grave. Are you familiar with Sisyphus?"

"That sounds like something an ill-kempt courtesan gave me this one time on Corsica," Donatello said, wincing at the memory.

Bardo's laughter echoed through the bar. He eventually settled down and said, "He was a Greek king long ago. After angering many gods for being arrogant, they made him spend eternity pushing a giant rock up a steep hill."

Donatello commented, "Couldn't we all say we're pushing a giant rock up a steep hill? Look at me. I'm searching for the perfect card hand, the best wine, and a talented whore I can make my wife. And you, dear Bardo, you're engaged in a futile battle to defeat me in cards. But like the Greek rock king's situation, some things are just life." He placed his cards on the table. "And that's a good hand," he said.

Bardo bit his lip in frustration. "Luck always sides with the new ones in Rome. Another hand?" he asked.

"Do I look like a bishop or cardinal?" joked Donatello.

"You must not know the cardinals who still owe me money," was Bardo's rejoinder.

Donatello flipped a gold coin in the air, saying, "When all is said and done, and all the cards have been dealt, and I have all your money, I guess I will take those debts over from you, my friend."

"Oh, you will?" asked Bardo, flinging his cards at Donatello angrily.

Chapter Ten

ROME, 1402

Every time Rome started a new settlement, a precise methodology always guided the general construction and layout. Originally arising out of army camps, Roman cities were built in a square grid. The general design became the nuclei of countless urban areas and synonymous with Roman expansion, but this concept did not apply to the actual city of Rome. The city's urban sprawl occurred organically in accordance with whatever space was available at the time, which is why the streets of Rome are more reminiscent of a knot set in stone. Somewhere out on the empty cobblestones Filippo found himself lost, but he was not afraid or worried in the least. Instead, he loved each moment, stepping further into the unknown; every nook and cranny attracted him like a moth to a flame.

Filippo followed a narrow road that opened into a square that had a stone water fountain. He approached the ledge, cupped his hand, and dipped it into the cold water. He took in his surroundings, in particular, the immaculately carved sculpture within the center of the fountain. From behind, a woman's voice broke through the still night air and said, "Her name's Fortuna."

The unexpected words startled Filippo and left him swaying on the fountain's ledge. The woman reacted without hesitation and pulled Filippo away from the water. But she pulled too hard, and the two landed on the ground on top of each other face to face.

"I'm so sorry," apologized Filippo, as he rolled off the woman, then helped her up off the ground.

She expressed regret as well. "I should have made my presence more apparent," she said.

Beneath the moon, Filippo caught a full glimpse of the woman. Her long, dark red hair instantly captivated Filippo and ignited his heart with dreams. He stared deep into her eyes and said, "Have I died and gone to heaven? For how else could I possibly be gazing on such an angel?"

His words made her cheeks blush as red as her hair, and she smiled coyly like a fox with a secret. She motioned to the fountain's center. "What I wanted to say was, that is Fortuna, the Roman goddess of luck."

Filippo smiled. "I do not believe in luck. Do you?"

"How else would you explain me saving you?" responded the woman.

"I call that fate," replied Filippo. "My name is Filippo. And you?"

The woman said, "Maria. And it was more like destiny."

Her name sounded like church bells ringing on Christmas morning to Filippo, and he asked her, "Pray tell, dear Maria, but why is a woman of such beauty out at such a late hour?"

"I came to beseech a wish from Fortuna at this fountain," answered Maria, who closed her eyes, held up a coin to her mouth, and kissed it. She extended her hand and dropped it into the water, then she looked back at Filippo. "Now, your turn."

He scoffed at her. "I told you I don't believe in that."

"I'll do it for you, if you don't have the coin," she said.

"I can do it myself," said Filippo stubbornly. He reached for his coin purse, opened it, then yelled, "Donatello!"

Maria asked, "Is everything okay?"

He revealed the contents of his pouch to her. "Does it look like it is?"

She laughed. "Are those wine corks?" she asked.

"They surely aren't my coins," responded Filippo.

"What are you going to do?" she asked.

"Oh, my best friend will pay, I promise you that. But I have to figure out where he is and where I am first."

Maria smiled back at him. "You're in Rome, my dear Filippo, the Eternal City."

On Rome's desolate streets, Filippo attempted to retrace his path back to the bar. But with each step, any and all thoughts of yelling at Donatello were replaced by images of Maria. Eventually, he had no idea where he was, but thinking about Maria eased his frustration. Moments later, his vision of Maria guided him to a street where he spotted Donatello and Bardo stumbling out of the bar.

"You thief!" screamed Filippo.

Bardo threw his hands up over his head and proclaimed his innocence, "I can explain!"

"Not you." Filippo pushed Bardo to the side, locking eyes with a drunk Donatello, and demanded, "Where is my money?"

Donatello sported a mischievous grin. "Huh? Oh, it's right here." He handed Filippo back his money, then reached into his pocket and revealed a handful of coins. Dropping the coins into

Filippo's hands, Donatello said to him, "I apologize. And this is your share of the profits."

Filippo looked bewildered at the coins. "My share?"

"That's your share," said Donatello, as Bardo mumbled something under his breath. Donatello smirked. "Don't mind Bardo. He thought the gods of fortune favored him upon this night. But nope, they do not. Instead, they pissed on him from above and extinguished all his luck."

"Where are you two off to?" inquired Filippo.

Donatello explained, "To get the rest of the money Bardo owes me. It appears our friend likes to bet big but without any coin to cover his losses."

Bardo crossed his arms and said, "I told you, I have your money back at my place. Just follow me there, and I will repay all my debts to you." He turned his back and began walking away.

As they hurried to catch up with him, Donatello asked, "How was your excursion?"

Filippo said, "I thought I died and met an angel, but she was actually a woman, a real one, the most beautiful one I have ever laid my eyes upon."

Donatello listened with attentive ears. "Interesting. And how did it go?"

"How am I to know?" said Filippo. "Some jackass put corks in my coin purse, so I had to abandon the girl of my dreams and rush back to the bar."

Donatello snickered at his answer and replied, "Filippo, you have been isolated in Florence for far too long. For even I know that jackasses do not lay eggs, let alone give birth to corks. Simply absurd."

Bardo guided the two friends through the complicated mess of turns and roads, eventually traversing the Tiber River on the

Ponte Fabricio, the oldest bridge in Rome, dating to 62 BC. On the other side, they hurried across Tiber Island and then another bridge, the Ponte Cestio. As Donatello pursued Bardo, Filippo noticed similar buildings as they went across Tiber Island once again.

"Maestro Bardo, are we nearing your residence? It seems as if you are leading us in circles," said Filippo.

"I got lost," barked back Bardo.

"My apologies. Please continue leading the way."

Walking away from the urban area, they were plunged into the darkness.

A few minutes later, Bardo stopped in front of ancient Roman ruins. Covered in sweat, Donatello fell to his knees in relief and commented, "I thought you lived in Rome, not past the edge of the world."

Filippo examined the surroundings and asked Bardo, "Is this Hadrian's Forum?"

"Who? I don't know him. Do you want your money or not?" grumbled Bardo.

The question revitalized Donatello, who answered, "I always want money, my friend."

Bardo said, "Good. Follow me," then he disappeared into the shadows.

Filippo pulled Donatello back. "Are you really just going to follow a stranger into the shadows?"

"He's no longer a stranger. He's a friend, a friend who owes me a lot of money. You already got your share, remember?" reminded Donatello.

Filippo motioned for him to lead the way. "After you."

As they progressed farther into the shadows, Bardo's voice attracted their attention, "Over here, my friend."

A distant torch guided them to Bardo on a grassy patch. In the flickering torchlight, Filippo realized that Bardo was standing in front of dug-up earth around a hole. Donatello glanced at the exposed hole in the ground and said, "My money must be down there."

Bardo quickly answered back, "Yes. All of your money is down there, my friend."

"Very well then, my friend," replied Donatello, who stepped up to the edge and promptly fell face first into the grave.

Filippo smacked his face with his palm when Donatello spoke up from the grave, "Could you hand me the torch, my friend? I can see only dirt."

Bardo brandished a knife, pointed it at Filippo, and said roughly, "Get in the grave with your friend. And I'm serious, dead serious."

Filippo scoffed. "I'm sure you and your pun are very serious, but I'm not getting in the grave," he countered.

"But I don't see any skeletons or anything," said Donatello.

"It's your grave, you *idiota*!" yelled Bardo.

"See, it belongs to Donatello, not me," pointed out Filippo.

Bardo screamed, "I'm going to stab you!"

"Absolutely not!" exclaimed Filippo, who leapt across the open grave to the other side.

"Oh, I will!" said Bardo, chasing Filippo around the grave.

Down below, Donatello realized he had a chance to rectify the situation. Standing on unsteady feet, he grabbed the closest leg he saw. However, the leg belonged to Filippo, and Donatello pulled him down into the grave too.

"I believe I made a mistake," apologized Donatello.

Filippo did not respond to his friend's admission, as Bardo screamed down into the grave, "Give me back my money!"

"Are you an *idiota*?" responded Filippo. "If you are, the answer is an obvious no, I will not give you back your money!"

Infuriated, Bardo sneered back, "Never say no to Bardo!" He dropped the torch and dove into the grave headfirst, holding the knife.

"Watch out!" yelled Filippo, as he pushed Donatello up against the dirt. Missing them, Bardo landed upright, face first in the dirt with the knife still in his hand.

"Is he dead?" asked Donatello.

A vengeful groan escaped Bardo. "No, but you are!" He pushed himself up from the soil but the ground gave way, sending all three careening into the darkness below.

Chapter Eleven

ROME, 1402

Moonlight cascaded down through the open grave, eventually reaching Filippo and illuminating his face. He lay on top of the pile of mud as more dirt was flung from above and landed on his face. He grimaced, then slowly sat up and groaned in pain, spitting out a mouthful of dirt. As he stood up, the moon briefly distracted him, until he recalled what had just happened. He frantically yelled out, "Donatello? Are you there?"

Donatello replied while scrabbling through the dirt on all fours, "I'll be better when I find my gold. It should be somewhere around here."

Filippo ignored his friend's words. Instead, glimpsing a dying torch on the ground, he summoned his remaining strength and leapt through the air. Despite landing hard on his stomach, Filippo grabbed the torch in time and held it upright. As the dwindling flames flared and spread on the torch, he let out a sigh of relief. Light soon fluttered around the room and revealed a collection of Corinthian columns and marble.

"No!" shrilled Donatello. "Bardo, my dear friend!" He rushed over to Bardo, who lay face down on the marble floor, and tried to shake him awake. "Please, dear friend, do not die! Your friendship provides the warmth of more than a hundred hearths!"

Filippo crossed his arms and griped, "Seriously? You do remember your friend tried to kill us. However, it looks like fate switched our places with his."

"How do you know he's dead? Couldn't he still be alive?" asked Donatello. "We survived the fall after all."

"Fine. Check to see if he's breathing, since he's your friend," said Filippo.

Donatello flipped Bardo onto his back and exposed a face flattened by marble. The gory sight made him relent, "I suppose you are right, Filippo. He looks beyond squashed. Plus, that is a rather large amount of blood to be leaking from someone's ears."

Filippo smiled. "The heavens favored us. We landed on the dirt, but he thankfully did not. And though the Coliseum may have smelled like the ass of a goat carcass rotting in the sun, at least it did not try to kill us."

Donatello said gloatingly, "True, but which choice left us with more coin in our pocket?"

Filippo jangled his purse. "You mean *I* was left with more coin. He never got around to paying *you*, dear friend."

Donatello quickly searched Bardo's pockets and found a hefty amount of coin, then yelled, "The liar had the money on him the whole time!" He delivered a swift kick to the corpse's ribs in retribution. But when his foot connected, fake cards flew up from Bardo's body.

"Looks like he was trying to cheat you too," pointed out Filippo. "But he got what was coming to him. Now we must find a way out of here before this becomes our grave too." Filippo wandered farther into the darkness, guided by the torch.

Donatello hobbled after him. "Wait. It feels as if I may have done something to my foot kicking that *bastardo* back there. And the surrounding shadows do not exactly seem inviting in the least."

The torchlight briefly revealed a darkened recess, which attracted Donatello's attention. Limping to the recess, he investigated, and said, "Filippo, bring the torch over here."

"What do you see? A door? Please, let it be a door," prayed Filippo.

Donatello responded, "No, it is something better."

A knee-high statue chiseled out of white marble rested beneath a layer of ancient dust. Donatello picked it up and wiped off dust and grime to reveal an exquisite sculpture of an attractive young woman draped in layers of linen. The sculpted marble depicted her garments blowing in the breeze. The superb display of craftsmanship amazed both artists.

Filippo broke the silence first and commented, "In all my years, I have never seen such skill."

"It's good. I'll give the sculptor that, but I can do better," boasted Donatello.

Torchlight guided the two artists deeper down a narrow hallway and farther into the unknown. They eventually found themselves in another room, this one much larger than the previous. Here, stacks of crates towered to the ceiling and an abundance of broken statues littered the ground. Filippo held the torch up to illuminate the relief of Jupiter. "If what remains of the Roman Forum is above our heads, we are in the storage rooms of the ancient temples," he said.

Donatello inspected his marble statue and asked, "What can you tell me about her?"

"Hold this and let me see," said Filippo, passing Donatello the torch. Holding the statue in his hands, he examined the woman's face in the light. "If I had to guess, she looks like a Vestal Virgin."

The answer took Donatello aback. "You do realize she's a sculpture, right? How can she know a man in that way, especially if she's a sculpture, Filippo? Answer me that?"

"Please, listen carefully, *idiota,*" instructed Filippo. "Vestal Virgins were selected virgins responsible for the hearth of the Roman state and making sure the sacred flames remained lit."

"Or what?"

"They'd be flogged," answered Filippo.

"What if a virgin was exceptionally gorgeous and found herself getting trumpeted by some man who could play the lyre?"

Filippo explained, "The Pontifex Maximus would condemn the unfortunate girl by burying her alive; yet others were sewed up in sacks filled with cats and thrown into the Tiber."

Filippo took back the torch and examined a nearby wall where stone debris blocked the doorway. "This must have been the way out, but not anymore."

Donatello's breath rate increased to panic mode. "What are we going to do? I can't die down here. I've got money to spend, wine to drink, and women to trumpet."

"Relax," assured Filippo. "I'm sure there's a way out."

While Filippo searched, Donatello leaned against a column. His weight nudged the column enough to push it over and it fell with a deafening crash. Clouds of dust filled the room, but when all settled, Filippo made his way over to Donatello and asked, "Are you okay?"

Donatello coughed back a reply, "We're both okay."

Standing on the edge of the massive hole created from the weight of the fallen column, Filippo spotted a chamber of carved stone. "There's another room beneath us," he said.

Donatello hobbled his way to the ledge. "And?"

"Hopefully, a way out," responded Filippo. He noticed Donatello supporting himself on the corner of a crate and asked, "Will you be able to make it?"

"Nothing some leeches should not be able to fix. Or better yet, a bottle of wine. And my dear friend, Filippo, I fail to see any wine down here, so let us leave with haste. But first, hold this again." Donatello handed the statue over to Filippo, stepped over the fallen column to straddle it, then scooted into the darkness below.

After descending the column, the two artists emerged into a narrow hallway carved out of vast deposits of volcanic rock called tufa. Cobwebs stretched from ceiling to floor filling the cramped space, but Filippo used the torch to ignite the webs. In a brief bright instant the webs combusted, rendering the pathway clear. Filippo took each step with caution as Donatello limped behind, clutching his marble statue.

Donatello's eyes soon adjusted to the darkness, when something appeared in his peripheral vision. He let out a murderous scream, "We're going to die!"

The words spun Filippo around, where he found Donatello shaking in fright and hiding behind his statue. Filippo pointed the torch into the shadows of a seemingly infinite recess. "It's only a catacomb," Filippo told Donatello, "and remember, *you're* the one who chose that particular bar where *you* met the murderer who brought us here."

Flustered, Donatello asked, "Are you always going to live in the past? You need to let things go, my dear friend."

The torch illuminated an ancient skull and disturbed a spider that climbed out of the orbital to escape back into the gloom. The lit recess also contained a worn scroll, left undisturbed for quite some time judging from the thick layer of dust suffocating it.

Donatello grabbed the scroll, wiped off the dust, and read the title with disappointment: "*De Architecture*. I was hoping it would be about spells or something worthwhile." Flipping through the pages, he commented, "It's nothing but a foolish scroll in Latin."

Filippo placed his hand over Donatello's mouth and said, "Shut up. And listen. Do you hear that?"

"Can I get a hint?" asked Donatello.

Filippo answered, "I hear flowing water, and you know what that means?"

Donatello shrugged and responded, "I don't really drink water. Does it have something to do with a fish?"

Filippo hurried ahead, carefully listening to each wall, but heard nothing. When he placed his ear on the floor, the sounds of trickling water made him smile. "It must be below us," exclaimed Filippo. Turning back to Donatello, he asked, "Can I borrow your statue for a second?"

Donatello gripped the statue tighter.

"I promise I'll give it right back," informed Filippo.

Donatello handed him the statue with uncertainty and asked him, "What are you going to do with it?"

"This." Filippo lifted the statue high above his head, then slammed it down into the ground.

"What are you doing to my woman?" yelled out an infuriated Donatello.

Filippo did not put it gently. "She's helping me dig our way out," he said.

Donatello snatched the statue back from Filippo and said, "If anyone is going to dig us out of my own bad decision, it's going to be me."

Filippo bowed out of the way and said, "Then by all means, please do so."

After several minutes of digging with the statue into the ground, Donatello broke through the tufa. He put his hands up in celebration, loudly pronouncing to all, "I did it! I saved the day!"

A noxious smell rose from the open hole and overtook Donatello's senses such that he vomited into the hole. Between violent fits of gagging, Donatello managed to speak, "It's as if the Coliseum somehow died and got buried beneath us. What type of black magic could do that?"

Filippo sniffed the air. "We must have broken into the Cloaca Maxima, which would surely explain the water and the smell."

Donatello complained, "But why does it smell like an ancient sewer?"

"That would be because it *is* one. Now, are you going to lead the way out?" asked Filippo.

Donatello stared down at the hole in the ground with intense concentration. The smell drifted upward from the sewer and he found himself fighting to keep from retching. Looking at Filippo through watery eyes, Donatello said, "I've lived a long and full life. I'll just crawl into one of those bunk bed graves on the wall and die. I'm not going down there."

"Are you done?" asked Filippo.

"Yes," replied Donatello.

Filippo smiled and said, "Good," then pushed Donatello into the sewer below with a splash.

Dating back to 600 BC, the Cloaca Maxima, or "Great Drain", helped redefine urbanization. What had originally been an open-air sewer built by Rome's prior inhabitants, the Etruscans, would be turned into a marvelous feat of Roman engineering. With urban space being at a premium due to the constantly growing population, one of the last kings of Rome, Tarquinius Priscus, ordered for construction directly over the open sewers, thus making the sewers underground. To prevent any structural collapse, Roman builders relied upon the use of the Roman arch below to reinforce the buildings sitting above. At a time when infectious disease was little understood and was believed to have a supernatural origin, the Roman sewers were vital for diverting waste away from the city for centuries. It was in these waters of Rome's past and present populations that Filippo and Donatello waded up to their knees, guided by a single torchlight.

Filippo raised the torch to keep the flames dry to guide their way. Meanwhile, Donatello did the same with his dirt-covered statue. Filippo soon stopped and studied something with the utmost focus. Donatello asked, "Are you all right up there? See anything? Like a staircase leading out?"

"Come stand by me," said Filippo.

Donatello stood shoulder to shoulder next to Filippo staring into the deep darkness before them, and asked, "What am I looking at?"

Filippo pointed to the bricks on the wall next to them. "See how these bricks appear this size, yet the ones disappearing into the distance gradually grow smaller despite the fact they are the same dimensions? However, if our eyesight moves by taking a step in either direction, the bricks still vanish, but the different vantage point creates a different perspective of seeing what is ultimately identical."

Tired, weary, and wounded, Donatello asked, "Do you even know where we're going?"

"The water's eventually going to flow to the Tiber," said Filippo, splashing his way forward.

Donatello scoffed. "Water? This is not water. Let's call it what it is. We're in sewage older than time immemorial. And darkness."

Raising the torch, Filippo countered, "Not total darkness. And I think I see our way out ahead. Or rather, over us."

Daylight came through the slivers of a manhole cover sitting above them.

Chapter Twelve

ROME, 1402

Although the immense wealth of the Medici family started in Florence, their financial holdings soon spread throughout European cities such as Geneva, Bruges, Avignon, and London, but first they would expand throughout the Italian peninsula. In the Campania region, they chose Naples on the western coast. To maximize profits, they also developed a Venetian branch in the northeastern region of Veneto. However, of all the branches the most financially profitable was the one located in Rome. With the city also serving as the center of Christendom, the Medici Bank found itself aligned with the Catholic Church by managing the monetary assets of the Holy See.

Giovanni di Medici needed someone he could trust to preside over such an important business venture. At first, he considered going himself, but he knew it would be unwise to leave the base of his banking operation. One day after discovering his sons Cosimo and Lorenzo fighting in the courtyard, he watched instead of intervening. Though Lorenzo put up a valiant effort, he could not match Cosimo's size or strength. Lorenzo knew which of his sons to send.

Cosimo di Medici arrived in Rome that morning after traveling straight from Florence in a painfully uncomfortable carriage. Before he could go rest at his family's Roman villa, he had to meet with Cardinal Odda Colonna. Their initial discussion pertained to how long their contract was, which the Cardinal Colonna felt was not long enough. Giovanni was more than happy to oblige and sent a document to the Cardinal Colonna through Cosimo extending their business relationship to the next quarter century.

After signing the contracts, Cardinal Colonna insisted on taking Cosimo to his favorite pizzeria. His father had told him how important this deal was and had insisted that he be cordial to all their clients. With a tired smile on his face, Cosimo followed Cardinal Colonna through the bustling streets of Rome in search of pizza.

"It must be around here somewhere," murmured Cardinal Colonna, spinning around in the middle of a congested street searching for the pizzeria.

Although he had only been in the city for hours, Cosimo knew they had been walking in circles. Keeping his mouth shut, he looked down at the well-traveled street surface. At first he thought his weary mind was tricking him when the manhole cover popped upward. But the second and third time proved to be real. Realizing that someone was trapped below, Cosimo quickly pried open the manhole cover and, to his surprise, pulled Donatello up from out of the darkness.

Donatello sat in the middle of the road, dripping with stagnating sewage. Clenching the marble statue firmly in his hands, he motioned back to the sewer and informed Cosimo, "There's one more down there."

Cosimo reached into the open hole and assisted Filippo up to the surface. Filippo thanked him. "You are a lifesaver, my friend. Wait, Cosimo?"

Shocked and surprised, Cosimo realized who it was and asked, "Filippo? What on earth are you doing in a Roman sewer?"

"Followed him to a bar last night," Filippo said, pointing at Donatello, who insisted on cleaning the statue rather than himself.

To avoid the foul odor of rotting excrement, the surrounding pedestrians took several steps back from Donatello. Only Cardinal Colonna stayed put, staring at the marble statue. The sheer exquisiteness of the work overcame the stench he sensed. "Your work appears to have been crafted by angels. Such a superb display of skill. I must have it," he demanded.

Gripping the statue tighter, Donatello stayed resolute and responded, "You can pray all you want for this, holy man. But the answer is no."

"Such insolence! But that is a trait displayed by all the great artists. I understand how hard it is to part with your work after investing time, emotion, and sacrifice to produce such a masterpiece. Would a hundred gold coins make you reconsider my request?" offered Cardinal Colonna.

"A hundred gold coins? Do you think of my talent as that worthless? My talent is priceless. Or at least it is worth a couple of small islands in a pleasant climate with vineyards, lots of vineyards."

Cosimo leaned into Filippo and asked, "The man your friend is mouthing off to, do you know who he is?"

Filippo shook his head, then Cosimo confessed, "That is Cardinal Colonna. According to my father, he holds the keys to the Catholic Church's vaults and a positive relationship can prove to be lucrative and beneficial for all involved."

"What does he do with the negative relationships?" asked Filippo.

Cosimo answered, "He prefers to subject them to a Persian torture called scaphism. The last man to anger him was placed in a hollow log with his limbs sticking out. Countless vases filled with honey and milk were poured into the log, and they left him on the banks of a swamp just north of the city."

"And?" inquired Filippo.

Cosimo shook his head in disgust. "You never want to hear the screams of a man being eaten alive by insects."

Hearing that, Filippo pulled Donatello up to his feet, pulled him off to the side, and delivered an ultimatum in hushed tones. "Either you're selling him that statue or you're going back into the sewer. Do you know why? Because if he gets mad, he feeds people to insects."

Donatello relented. "Fine," he said, handing the statue to Cardinal Colonna. "Is your offer still available?"

Cardinal Colonna tossed him a bag of gold coins and spoke, "There is plenty more if you can produce more statues of such high quality."

"I can produce works of such beauty that you will grow disillusioned with reality and gouge your eyes out," boasted Donatello.

Filippo approached Cardinal Colonna, saying, "But once we get a workshop set up, we can produce works like you have never seen before."

Cardinal Colonna smiled with great enthusiasm and said, "Follow me. I know just the place for you to work."

"He's *your* problem now," said Cosimo to Filippo, "I'm in dire need of some rest, but heed what I told you earlier."

After Cosimo departed, Cardinal Colonna walked with Filippo and Donatello to an empty building a short distance away. Located off a hidden road, the two-storied structure appeared to have survived every riot, battle, and coup throughout Rome's history. The original concrete façade was gone and all that was left was traces of exposed and weathered brick. Cardinal Colonna opened the door. "After you."

Inside they walked into an empty workspace with high, vaulted ceilings. "I apologize for the lack of furnishings and supplies, but I can have those items brought here within the week. The previous tenant was a particularly special friend of a late bishop, who felt he misplaced his trust in her. So she happened to have her head misplaced. And upon that note, I have other business to which I must attend. But I will return soon to see what you are making."

With Cardinal Colonna's departure, Filippo glanced at Donatello. "You realize he is expecting us to produce more works like that."

"All we have to do is go back down to that lair of smells and get more statues," mused Donatello. "It will not be that hard. In fact, I plan on doing it when I am very drunk."

"What happens when we run out of statues?" wondered Filippo.

"When that happens, I hope we will be producing sculptures like those of the past. It's called ambition and setting high standards, like really high in this case," surmised Donatello. "Oh, I forgot I have a gift for you." He fished into his pocket and revealed *De Architecture*, the scroll from the catacombs. "It's all in Latin and I have no use for it."

~

That evening Donatello opted to visit another tavern. However, Filippo declined the invitation and wandered the streets of Rome, admiring the buildings. Standing before a decimated house with only a partial frame and front wall remaining, something caught his attention, so he scribbled a quick sketch in a notebook. Looking over his shoulder to make sure no one was around, Filippo grabbed some of the weakened façade and pried it off. Behind the exterior, thin bricks were situated in a unique herringbone pattern. He placed his finger on one of the upper bricks and traced the pattern of structural force, which went down and to the side at ninety degrees, then back down again and repeated. He copied the herringbone design in his notebook.

Around the next turn Filippo entered an open square with a flowing fountain. He sated his thirst with the cool mountain water delivered by the aqueducts as he first gazed upon the Pantheon. Quarried from Egypt, a forest of Corinthian columns formed the entrance, each standing close to forty feet in height and five feet in diameter. Massive letters adorned the outward face, letting all who entered know that Marcus Agrippa had built it during the third consulate in 27 BC to celebrate the victory at the Battle of Actium. Within a century, fires would raze the structure to the ground. But under Emperor Hadrian's rule in 125 AD, construction began to restore the "Temple to the Gods" back to prominence.

Filippo ambled in a state of reverent curiosity through the portico surrounded by the towering columns. Emerging into the rotunda, his eyes were immediately drawn to the domed roof and then to the Pantheon's only natural light source, the Oculus, the massive opening in the roof. The architectural combination left Filippo breathless. His hands rapidly scribbled down aspects of the ancient temple, until a familiar voice called out, "Were you able to get your money back?"

Filippo spotted the woman from the previous night, Maria, strolling into the rotunda. "The heavens smiled upon me that night in many ways, for I am still breathing. And I can see they still do," he said.

"Breathing is always a good thing," asserted Maria. "What brings you to the Pantheon at such a late hour?"

"I was merely enjoying the fine wonders of Rome when my breath was taken away," mused Filippo.

Maria agreed. "The Pantheon has that ability," she said.

"Oh, I was talking about you," said Filippo.

Maria blushed. After composing herself, she spoke, "Supposedly, when Pope Boniface IV entered here in the seventh century, he believed the ceiling to represent heaven in its uniform pattern of perfection. This would be the first Roman temple to be converted. No other would be for centuries, which shows how impressive and remarkable this place truly is."

Filippo listened to Maria's voice echo through the interior and he said, "How can a building of such magnitude be so empty?"

Maria smiled. "I don't mind that it's just the two of us. But if you must know, we're not alone."

"We're not?"

Maria shook her head. "No. After consecrating the Pantheon, Boniface ordered for wagonloads of martyrs to be removed and interred beneath the altar." Spotting his sketchbook, she asked, "Do you mind?"

Filippo reluctantly handed it to her. He waited nervously as she flipped through the pages and she said, "Your drawings appear so realistic, as if the pictures jump off the page and can be touched. Other works appear so flat and dull, yet your drawings capture what my eyes truly see."

Church bells rang out, echoing through the streets of Rome and flowing into the Pantheon. Upon hearing them, Maria apologized, saying, "The hour is getting quite late, and I must return to my home. Perhaps we'll run into each other again."

As she exited, Filippo admired the Oculus, then spoke out loud, "Heaven was indeed witnessed within these walls tonight."

Chapter Thirteen

Displaying the enthusiasm of a young man, a jovial Cardinal Colonna hurried up to the door of Filippo's workshop. Instead of knocking, he glanced back over his shoulder and called out, "I'm the one nearly at death's doorstep. Now, hurry up, boy."

Cardinal Colonna had waited for months for this day to arrive. Over a decade ago the Papacy had left its confines within St. Peter's because of the plague outbreak ravaging Rome. During this absence, Cardinal Colonna relied upon his intelligence, social connections, and everything else at his disposal to mastermind his meteoric rise through the Vatican ranks. Now he walked the streets of Rome as one of the city's most powerful men. With the vast Vatican coffers at his disposal, Cardinal Colonna took it upon himself to remodel and update St. Peter's, telling people that his efforts were to accommodate the Pope upon his return. However, even the blind poet Homer, who had died centuries ago in Greece, could see that it was Cardinal Colonna's personal interests and tastes that guided all the remodeling.

Ever since first gazing upon the sculpture of the Vestal Virgin, Cardinal Colonna had developed an obsession with antiquity and its forgotten splendors. To help satiate his artistic passion, he employed the services of Filippo and Donatello. Their work consisted of a mix of authentic, original pieces inspired by the past, and they also passed Roman sculptures off as their own; regardless, Cardinal Colonna could not tell the difference and paid well. But on that day, the Cardinal wanted art that made all previous work pale in comparison, at least in the Cardinal's judgment.

Although many years Cardinal Colonna's junior, Cosimo di Medici lagged more than several paces behind. When Cosimo reached the door, he gasped and said, "I shall never underestimate your spryness again, Cardinal."

Cardinal Colonna's equally spry intellect was responsible for his political ascent, which would never have been possible without financial assistance from the Medici Bank. Early on, he recognized how vital and instrumental an alliance with such an institution could be over time. But when his prediction came to fruition, even he was surprised at how often the Medici Bank filled the Vatican vaults.

"Your livelihood is that of finance, mine is staying ahead of not just my enemies but my friends as well," smiled Cardinal Colonna as he knocked on the hardwood door with his bejeweled knuckles.

Squeaks accompanied an opening door with rusty hinges. Filippo appeared in the doorway beaming with delight. "Cardinal Colonna and Cosimo, please enter, my good friends," he said.

"As always, it would be my pleasure," declared Cardinal Colonna.

Cosimo followed Cardinal Colonna into the workshop, when he suddenly remembered something. He presented Filippo with a decayed manuscript on the verge of total deterioration. "I almost forgot that this is for you. You remarked how much you enjoyed translating those Latin scrolls, so I thought you might like this."

As Filippo accepted the manuscript with delicate hands, Cardinal Colonna mentioned, "You should transcribe that as you read. It's quite old and would not surprise me in the least if merely reading it will cause it to wither into a pile of dust."

"Who wrote it, if I may ask?" inquired Filippo.

Cosimo handed the scroll over and answered, "Don't ask me. You're the one who can read Latin."

Filippo's finger underlined the author's name, as he read out loud, "Pee-Too-Lee-Me."

Cardinal Colonna rolled his eyes, saying, "It was written by one of the greatest minds ever to walk upon Earth, Ptolemy."

Filippo smiled to hear the name. "Wait, is this founder of the Ptolemaic Dynasty?" he asked.

"Same lineage, but this one came around four and a half centuries later," smiled Cardinal Colonna.

"If he's so great, then how come he's dead?" remarked Cosimo. "Is Donatello here? I need to rehydrate my brain with some wine."

Filippo spun around and said, "Follow me. I believe he's in the back."

They walked by dozens of unfinished projects. Sculptures varied in size from petite to colossal; some made of wood, some of marble, and others an amalgamation of each with a marble façade. "There it is!" exclaimed Cardinal Colonna.

In a back corner, Donatello was polishing a brilliant blue marble sculpture. "And now it is ready," declared Donatello, as he presented an immaculately carved Italian greyhound to the Cardinal.

Ever since he was a boy Cardinal Colonna had adored Italian greyhounds. Years ago, he had found a constant companion in a particular stray greyhound he adopted and named Leon. The prized dog had been his companion until a year ago, when Leon succumbed to an illness. Cardinal Colonna mourned for quite some time but now stood holding a sculpture immortalizing his beloved furry friend. "As if it were formed from the blue heavens above," he said rapturously.

On a nearby wall, sketches hung on a wall and covered a table and the mess attracted Cosimo's attention. Each piece was an architectural sketch detailing some unique structural aspect of a Roman building from multiple perspectives. "Donatello, does this paper nest belong to you?" asked Cosimo.

"Little kids scribble like that. Adults like myself create with our hands," admonished Donatello. "That rat nest belongs to Filippo; ask him."

Outside, church bells rang out and woke Cardinal Colonna from his trance. "I must get going to oversee evening Mass for some foreign diplomats. Thank you again for all your hard work and talents," he announced, placing two bags of gold on a table. Walking out, Cardinal Colonna said, "More will be arriving in the morning."

Filippo left via a side room, struggling to hold a statue of a Roman goddess in his arms. "Cardinal? Are you here?" he asked.

"He had holy appointments to keep," said Cosimo. "Are these your drawings?"

Filippo set the statue down and wiped the sweat from his brow. "They are nothing more than some interesting features adorning Roman buildings."

"Stop being modest, Filippo. You've dissected, rearranged, deconstructed, and reconstructed almost every building in this city," said Donatello.

"Every place except the Pantheon," admitted Filippo, "but her secrets will be revealed tonight."

"While you are deconstructing that ruin of a temple, I'll be at a tavern deconstructing a woman out of her clothes to get into *her* temple," Cosimo joked.

Donatello blurted out, "That sounds like fun. Do you need any assistance with that, my dear friend, Cosimo?"

"You can meet up with him after we measure," Filippo said. "Last time you were so drunk that you got tangled up in the measuring rope and kept tripping until finally passing out behind one of the columns."

"Let's be honest, that place has been there for almost forever; surely it will be there tomorrow or the next day or the day after," Donatello reminded him.

"As will the taverns. The sooner we finish, the sooner you can join Cosimo at the tavern," wheedled Filippo.

Donatello walked toward the door. "Then why are we still here?" he asked.

As the evening sun was setting, Filippo and Donatello sat on the ledge of the fountain and stared at the Pantheon before them. "Since I'm assisting you in this endeavor in a state of somewhat partial sobriety, you must answer just one question," asked Donatello.

Filippo responded, "And what would you like to know?"

"Why do you come here almost every day? I don't see the appeal."

"There's something about it. In any attempt to explain, words fail to do it proper justice. The entire experience, from entering through the columns to the sublime representation within, seems to keep me in a constant state of wonderment," answered Filippo.

Donatello thought about that, then said, "Whatever it is, it involves a woman. That much I know. No man speaks like that unless there is a woman somehow in the equation."

Inside the Pantheon's rotunda, Filippo measured out a knotted rope with equal increments then tossed it across the room to Donatello. But the rope fell far short. Walking to retrieve it, Donatello pouted. "Are we done yet?"

"Almost. Make sure to pull out any excess slack," instructed Filippo. "I need the measurement to be as exact as possible."

"I honestly thought Rome would have expanded your hobbies beyond that of meticulous measurements, but no, here we are," chastised Donatello.

Without even looking up from recording the data, Filippo responded, "That coming from a man with a preferred hobby of drinking until all moral behavior and bladder control is expunged. Please remind me again of the exact difference between your activities in Rome and Florence?"

"Here in Rome, when I venture into any tavern, it seems as if everyone knows me for me and my talents," asserted Donatello. "People walk up asking if I am the artist who created this work or that work. Florence stifled my further artistic progression. Being there simply limited my talents. Plus, I can charge my drinking expenses to Cardinal Colonna's tab."

"But you did the same thing in Florence to the Wool Merchants' Guild," remarked Filippo.

"True, but here in Rome, Cardinal Colonna is fully aware I am charging his tab. In fact, he was the one who insisted I do so. He felt uneasy with the amount of coin I had to take with me to cover my drinking expenses," mused Donatello, "but alas, instead of seeing how deep the Vatican coffers go, I am here." Gazing up at the dome, he followed the geometric pattern to the Oculus in the ceiling's middle and wondered out loud, "Did they mean to do that?"

Filippo walked along the taut rope counting the knots and recording them on parchment. Satisfied, he kneeled down and collected the rope. "Only one way to find out."

Moments later, Filippo and Donatello were outside staring up at the vertical wall on the side of the portico. Donatello turned to Filippo and said, "Race you to the top."

Filippo responded by firmly gripping a ledge and pulling himself upward. Not to be outdone, Donatello scrambled up the wall adjacent to him. As the warm day gave way to the cool evening air, the two friends soon found themselves near physical exhaustion three-quarters of the way up.

"We should have used the rope," lamented Donatello, struggling to maintain his balance.

"Hold on," instructed Filippo as he made his way up the side.

Donatello snapped back, "Trust me. I am holding on for my life, for I have no intention of joining our late friend Bardo and being flattened by a fall."

Filippo stopped his ascent, turned back down to Donatello, and complained, "He was *your* friend. I always hated him." Upon saying that, Filippo pulled himself up on the portico's angled roof. After securing the rope around a barred gutter drain, he returned to the ledge and dropped the rope down to Donatello.

A steady stream of profane language accompanied Donatello's climb. After reaching the top, he nearly collapsed and complained, "I would say I owe you my life, but your insane desire for measurements placed it in danger to start."

"The climb is often the most grueling part," said Filippo, offering Donatello a hand up.

Donatello snapped, "Despite straddling life and death after that climb, I heard that."

Confused, Filippo asked, "You heard what?"

"You said *often*, and that means exceptions," asserted Donatello. "What exceptions remain for your measurements? What's left? Another perilous climb to the heavens? Maybe fight some dragons? Or deal with an annoying Frenchwoman? If it is any of those, then I choose the climb or dragons over the Frenchwoman. The last one I knew kept nagging, me, 'Donatello, you relieved yourself on my parents' priceless rug,' 'Donatello, you slept with my best friend,' 'Donatello, you slept with my sister.' I'll take a fatal climb to my death or a duel with a dragon any day over that mistake."

"How does your mind reach such rambling conclusions?" asked Filippo.

Donatello shrugged. "Probably from the dire lack of the wine my body needs to function properly."

Church bells rang out in the distance. Filippo heard them and responded, "Are you serious? We've been here for almost an hour."

Filippo led Donatello up to the apex of the portico's roof, then they climbed up to the exterior of the Pantheon's dome. On the flat surface above the entrance, they faced the five concentric circles. Filippo examined how the bricks lined the exterior of the lowest and widest circle, then jotted down the information.

Donatello walked up the circles to the actual dome, where he scrambled up the angled side and looked down through the Oculus into the interior of the rotunda.

Filippo worked his way up the dome to the Oculus across from Donatello, then tossed him the rope. While they straightened the rope for an exact measurement, Donatello remarked, "It's much bigger than it looks from below."

"Shame that is not what the girls in the brothels tell you," chuckled Filippo, as he wrote down the diameter of the Oculus.

"Quicker you get done, quicker I can find out," said Donatello, as he turned his attention away from the Pantheon to the magnificent city of Rome surrounding him.

Filippo dropped an end of the rope down through the Oculus. While pulling the rope up, he meticulously counted the knots. "It appears that whoever built this knew how to incorporate symmetry into the design. The height of the Oculus matches perfectly with the rotunda's interior."

Filippo produced a short-bladed knife and proceeded to chisel samples of concrete from each layered circle. "Deciding to leave your own mark?" commented Donatello.

"It's to determine the structural formation," replied Filippo, as he placed each sample in a specific pocket.

Back at the workshop, Filippo found himself working diligently by candlelight trying to interpret the trove of information he had collected from the Pantheon. After amassing the structure's various measurements, Donatello excused himself and stumbled to the taverns to meet up with Cosimo. Filippo was thankful his friend's drunken debauchery took him somewhere aside from the workshop, as Donatello's absence allowed for Filippo to concentrate without any interruptions.

Filippo carefully set out the collected samples of concrete from the Pantheon, each one varying in where it was placed on the structure. After pouring water from a pitcher into a bowl, he placed some concrete collected from the columns supporting the portico into the water. Within seconds, the concrete sank to the bottom of the bowl. Next, he placed the sample gathered from the rotunda into the bowl. To his surprise, that particular concrete floated on top of the water's surface. When Filippo pressed the sample to the bottom of the bowl, the concrete's buoyancy propelled it back to the surface. As he recorded his finding, Donatello barged in, drunk and rambunctious.

"Filippo! Guess what? I got drunk. Shocking, I know," slurred Donatello. "Missed out on a fun night."

"It is all fine, my friend, for I may have figured out how the Pantheon still stands," said Filippo, as he refocused on his work.

"Magic?" answered Donatello. "Usually, that's the answer I give when I don't know something. You'd be surprised how many people agree."

Filippo rolled his eyes. "What appears to be magic to some is nothing more than knowledge and information for others. It seems as if those who built the Pantheon specifically decreased the weight as they went upward. The concrete around the Oculus is much lighter than the denser concrete used at the base."

Hearing a crash echo throughout the workshop, Filippo looked up from his notes to discover Donatello passed out on the ground; his deafening snores echoed through the workshop. Filippo returned to his work when someone knocked at the door.

"Who could be awake at this hour? Besides me, of course," wondered Filippo, as he opened the door to find a courier.

"Are you Filippo Brunelleschi?" asked the courier.

"That I am," Filippo answered. "How may I be of service at this late hour?"

"Then this message belongs to you," said the courier as he removed a sealed envelope from his satchel and handed it to Filippo.

Filippo accepted the letter but focused more on his notes. He returned to his desk and placed the letter on it, then resumed his structural analysis of the Pantheon. As the night wore on, pieces of scrap paper eventually covered the letter.

Weeks would pass, eventually becoming months, before spilled wine forced Filippo to attend to his cluttered work desk. In an effort to salvage his notes, he frantically hung each piece of paper on a piece of rope. Beneath the crimson-stained paper he discovered the courier's letter dripping in wine. He briefly debated whether to toss it into the fire, but curiosity overcame him. After opening the envelope with a penknife, he found the letter within remarkably dry. Filippo flung the ruined envelope into the flames, then began to read the letter.

The words on the page overwhelmed Filippo. He staggered to find a place to sit, but his legs gave out and he collapsed to the workshop's floor. He buried his face in his hands and bellowed out a grief-stricken moan.

Chapter Fourteen

FLORENCE, 1417

Due to the political aspirations of King Ladislaus of Naples, Cosimo di Medici fled the city of Rome and found himself back in his hometown of Florence. Although he wrote to his father suggesting he stay and preside over their financial affairs, Giovanni di Medici knew the risks. With their family's vast wealth growing at a nearly exponential rate, so did the envy and jealousy of their enemies, and most especially of their friends. However, by having someone trusted in Rome like his son, Giovanni stood to gain an unfathomable amount of financial influence over Europe and Christendom. But placing a family member outside of the Florentine walls meant potential kidnappings or worse, all of which could compromise everything the Medici patriarch had constructed carefully over the years. Cosimo understood his father's judgment concerning his welfare, but even so, he loathed the restriction forced upon him and often compared his life to that of an imprisoned captive void of free will.

When word reached him that his dear friend Filippo Brunelleschi was also in Florence, Cosimo set out that morning to visit the Brunelleschi household. The last time Cosimo had seen Filippo was years ago in Rome. One morning, Cosimo and Donatello had returned to their workshop after a night of debauchery at the taverns. Every morning, Filippo would be at his desk cursing under his breath as he interpreted and transcribed some forgotten architectural treatises. He was a familiar sight as the sun rose, except for that morning. Filippo's messy work desk was clean. No pieces of scrap paper scribbled with notes or a quick sketch could be seen, only a folded note addressed to Donatello. Cosimo remembered watching Donatello read it, then turn toward him looking upset and saying, "It appears Filippo left. And he will not be coming back."

Cosimo still remembered the first time he laid eyes upon Filippo since Rome and the uncertainty and the fear he had experienced then. After being greeted at the front door by Filippo's mother, Giuliana, he followed her up the stairs. Reaching the top, she turned to Cosimo with a trembling lip teetering on the verge of sobbing. As she fought to regain composure, a quiet "Thank you" escaped her mouth.

"My family and I are here for you and your children in any capacity," said Cosimo.

With a gentle knock on a door, Giuliana announced their presence, saying, "Filippo, you have a guest."

As they entered the room, Cosimo took note of the darkness that blanketed everything except for a dim light from a single window that revealed Filippo's pale, gaunt body lying in bed. Cosimo realized that the fragile shell was his friend and he smiled and said, "It's been quite some time, old friend."

Filippo turned his head at the remark and responded with a expression reminiscent of a mortally wounded animal. He said apologetically, "I should have thought that through."

Cosimo's visit lasted no longer than half an hour and he left feeling as if his attempt to help his old friend had done more harm than good. Despite Filippo not responding with words, Giuliana noticed that his face had shown traces of appreciation for the visit. At her insistence, Cosimo visited again later that week. The second time appeared to be as productive as the first. But when Cosimo described the agony of meeting with drunken cardinals to discuss bank loans, he referenced a humorous anecdote involving some cardinals who relieved themselves off balconies onto onlookers below, at which Filippo chuckled a little. With a simple joke, some of the haze in Filippo's eyes seemed to dissipate. On each successive visit to Filippo, Cosimo tried to make his friend smile or laugh at least once.

A roaring fireplace heated the massive great room of the Palazzo Medici on a brisk autumn night. Cosimo warmed himself up by the fire, as his father, Giovanni, sat at the end of a table crossing out names on a list.

Cosimo assured his father, "I saw what he was capable of in Rome. A genius such as him does not come along so often."

"What of his condition?" inquired Giovanni. "Ever since the passing of his father, murmurings of Filippo's decline have been incessant."

"His father died, and word did not reach him for some time," revealed Cosimo. "The torment of trying to fill such an absence, when nothing can, created his anguish and turmoil. Each time I visit him, his condition improves. The old Filippo is still there, I know it, but hidden behind self-imposed despair."

"He showed such promise during the contest for the Baptistery doors. A talent like his has the potential to either make the project or completely devastate it. What if he experiences another hardship along the way? Will he simply go hide under his sheets, locked away from the world?" wondered Giovanni.

Cosimo reminded his father, "Before that happens, he must succeed in earning the panel's approval and surely show some foresight in his approach. But for all I know, he might respond with a disdainful stare."

"After some of the proposals today, disdain might be a reasonable approach," remarked Giovanni snidely.

The next day, Cosimo left his family's residence and headed straight to see Filippo. As usual, Giuliana greeted him at the door and led him up to Filippo's chambers. Filippo was sitting up in bed but still appeared somewhat despondent when they entered his room. Seeing Filippo sitting up on his own brought Giuliana to tears. Cosimo took his regular seat by the bed and spoke as if the two old friends were back in Rome at Filippo's workshop. "If you are feeling up to it, we have need of your talents, friend. I was discussing potential names with my father, and I immediately thought that no one is capable of completing this but you. However, you will need to impress a panel with a design to obtain the contract first."

For the first time in years, Filippo spoke, "There are countless others, all of whom show skill and talent far exceeding anything I am capable of doing."

Cosimo placed a piece of folded parchment on a table near Filippo, saying, "For when curiosity gets the better of you." Then he left the room.

That night in front of the great hearth at the Palazzo Medici, Giovanni asked, "Cosimo, how did your attempt at retrieving Filippo from Purgatory go?"

"In some aspects, it surpassed all preconceived notions," answered Cosimo.

A pleasant smile formed on Giovanni's face, and he inquired, "I take it then Filippo will be vying for the contract?"

"Oh, of that part I am still unsure. However, he did speak today with actual words," exclaimed Cosimo.

"As it appears he has regained the ability to speak, perhaps I should pay him a visit?" suggested Giovanni.

The following morning, Giovanni decided to forgo his usual breakfast of smoked duck and sweet honey-glazed rolls and get a jumpstart on his day. Having not journeyed to the Santa Maria Novella district in quite some, he wanted to allow time for any possible congestion upon the Florentine streets. Meetings filled his day, and the wisdom that comes with age taught him it was better to start early than late.

After arriving at Filippo's house much earlier than intended, Giovanni knocked on the door with a thunderous clang loud enough to wake up everyone on the block. The door opened to reveal Cassandra, Filippo's sister, eating a bowl of porridge. From his clothes, she could tell that a man of means stood before her and she asked, "Do you need assistance?"

Giovanni cleared his throat and stated, "Yes, my good dear, I am here to talk with Filippo Brunelleschi."

His statement startled Cassandra and left her at a loss for words, then she stuttered back a reply, "Please wait here," and closed the door.

Shortly later, Giuliana reopened the door, but before she could open her mouth Giovanni said, "I must talk to Filippo."

"And who may I announce for this visit?" inquired Giuliana.

"Giovanni di Medici."

As the morning sun spilled light that erased the night's shadows, Giuliana led him up to Filippo's room and tapped on the door, asking, "Filippo, are you awake? You have a visitor."

Without even hearing a reply, Giovanni took it upon himself to enter the gloomy room. Giovanni loudly ordered Giuliana, "Please leave and return with at least two dozen candles and a dozen green plants. This room appears to be confined to permanent midnight, and that will not do."

Filippo sat up in his bed and asked, "Giovanni?"

"Wonderful! Your memory still works," smiled Giovanni.

Without raising his voice, Filippo demanded, "Why are you here?"

"To recover potential greatness from seeping further into the abyss. Cosimo kept me fully informed of your exploits in Rome, in particular, your desire to rediscover all that has been lost since antiquity," explained Giovanni. Eyeing the letter left by Cosimo sitting open on Filippo's bed, he remarked, "Would you like to be remembered as what could have been? Or would you like your greatness to be cemented above in the sky for all of Florence, for all of Italy, and for the world to stare on in astonishment? The choice belongs to you, son, and no one else can make it but you."

As Giovanni walked out of the room, he turned back to Filippo and spoke, "Greatness is a choice that always requires effort. A man may be born to obscurity, but through intelligent practice and diligent application, his legacy will be fulfilled and be everlasting."

Late at night, surrounded by plants and candlelight, Filippo rummaged through a chest overflowing with various notes and drawings from his Roman tenure. He organized each piece in accordance with the topic; soon, piles pertaining to the Pantheon and translations of ancient treatises formed on his table.

A gentle rapping at his door caused Filippo to look up for the first time in hours. Giuliana stood smiling in the doorway holding a plate of fish for his dinner. "I saw the candlelight beneath your door and thought you might be hungry," she said sweetly.

Smelling the food, Filippo remembered that he was hungry. He graciously accepted the plate, saying, "It's as if you read my mind. What is it?"

"Smoked herring," she responded before leaving the plate between the stacks of notes on his table.

Some time later, Filippo cut into the herring's back, revealing steaming white meat and bones. As he pierced the herring's meat with a fork, he observed the unique pattern of the herring's spinal column, its zigzagging vertebral design. Comparing the two, Filippo had an epiphany and he furiously wrote his revelation down in a state of total immersion.

Chapter Fifteen

FLORENCE, 1418

Florentines saw an open eyesore each time they looked up at the unfinished ceiling of Santa Maria del Fiore, which made them very resentful of city administrators. Giovanni quickly recognized the situation, which he saw as an opportunity to further expand his family's influence and legacy. Yet he knew the risks of financing such a project would be too great for him to take on by himself. To limit any potential monetary loss, Giovanni approached the Arte della Lana, the Wool Merchants' Guild of Florence. Although Cosimo urged his father to postpone the design competition for his friend Filippo, no more delays were possible because the citizens of Florence demanded a roof on their beloved cathedral.

One late November day, Giovanni found himself sitting at the luxurious Palazzo Vecchio adjacent to his two sons, Cosimo and Lorenzo. He was supposed to be listening to an architect named Dion from Arsoli but instead found himself fighting the urge to fall asleep. "I promise you the greatest dome in all the land," said Dion, before bowing deeply to the panel before him.

Also at the table sat Piero, a high-ranking wool merchant, who asked Dion, "And how will you accomplish this?"

Dion bowed again and responded, "With your money, of course."

The response flustered Giovanni, who grumbled back, "Do you have any plans, boy? We want to see some course you will follow before we let you run amok in our coffers. For all we know, you might plan to build the dome with invisible bricks fashioned from air or some rubbish."

Dion thought for a moment, then spoke, "I am a skilled bricklayer from Arsoli, and I, Dion from Arsoli, have completed many projects, too many to even recollect and name."

"Can you give me one?" asked Giovanni.

Dion shrugged. "There are just so many."

Giovanni rolled his eyes, then flipped through a stack of papers and dredged up a single parchment. After carefully reading it to himself, he inquired, "Are you the same Dion from Arsoli that is wanted for shoddy construction? According to this document, you are still wanted by the Arsoli authorities for the deaths of multiple individuals after one of your many projects collapsed. Do you have anything to say to those charges?"

"Would you believe it was my brother? He's full of hate and evil and does not understand construction like me, the good brother," pleaded Dion.

Giovanna dismissed him by yelling, "Next!"

As the next builder entered the room vying for the right to finish the cathedral, Giovanni saw that both Cosimo and Lorenzo were each lost somewhere in a nap. Giovanni lamented, "If only we could switch places."

"What is your name?" Piero asked the builder.

The man cleared his throat, then spoke, "I am the great designer Olinda. Perhaps you have heard of me?"

Those on the panel who were still awake turned to the others and shrugged in unison. "Clearly, no one here has. But get on with it," rambled Giovanni.

Olinda cracked his knuckles and said, "First, I will need enough scaffolding."

"Next!" yelled Giovanni.

"Next?" responded a confused Olinda. "But I just started my presentation. I have yet to show you my proposal. Would you like to hear it?"

"Not really, truth be told," answered Giovanni. He locked eyes with Olinda and asked, "Have you ever seen the dome?"

Olinda shook his head from side to side.

"Clearly," said Giovanni. "The scaffolding you demand would take centuries to grow. We would have to decimate almost every forest from here to the Alps simply to have enough wood. So, that begs the question: Can you do it without any scaffolding?"

Olinda gathered his belongings. "I'll see myself out."

Piero turned to Giovanni and groaned. "Do you think they realize the scope of the project at hand? It seems to me they all are each soundly convinced their partially conceived ideas can actually succeed." But his peripheral vision caught someone entering the room, and Piero addressed him, "Are you the next one to be rejected?"

Filippo glared at him and said, "I am the final one."

Piero rolled his eyes. "Wonderful. Another one with an ego so big, all of Tuscany is at risk of sinking."

Hearing the condescending tone, Filippo lashed back, "Lucky for us all, one cannot measure your stupidity in weight, or we all would surely have drowned beneath the waves quite some time ago."

"Filippo!" shouted Giovanni in an effort to save Filippo from himself. "Seeing you out of bed eases my worries," he said, then turned to Piero. "Have you ever met Filippo Brunelleschi?"

Piero lifted his nose in disdain. "I can't say I have had the pleasure. Who is he?" he asked archly.

"So, now you can brag to everyone that you know him," taunted Filippo. "Now, for those in charge, let us commence the act of me securing that contract."

The verbal onslaught roused Cosimo and Lorenzo from their naps. Cosimo rubbed his eyes and said, "Filippo? Is that you?"

"I apologize for disturbing your sleep, but I need to impress the panel," replied Filippo.

Cosimo smiled delightedly. "It's quite all right. Oh, did you know I'm on the panel?" he asked.

"Oh, I meant those that make the actual decisions on the panel," insisted Filippo. Giovanni erupted in laughter.

Piero spoke over the laughter sharply to Filippo. "And why should such a prestigious job be granted to a braggadocio when in reality you are nothing but a failed goldsmith?"

"Oh, then you have heard of me, *signore*," said Filippo patronizingly. "Please refrain from lying in the future, as your dishonesty might compromise the integrity of such a noble pursuit as finishing the House of God."

As Piero raged beneath his calm exterior, Giovanni motioned for Filippo to proceed with his bid. Filippo walked up to the table. An egg appeared in his hand. "Please stand this egg upright," instructed Filippo.

"This is absurd! What does an egg have to do with architecture?" demanded Piero.

Filippo calmly responded, "It has everything to do with architecture. Why? Because shapes are natural."

Meanwhile, Giovanni struggled to balance the egg upright but the egg wobbled and fell to its side. "I give up," he professed and passed the egg to Lorenzo.

"I think I remember this trick from childhood," proclaimed Lorenzo. He shook the egg, placed it on its end, but it still tipped over.

Cosimo took the egg, studied it carefully, and attempted to balance it on its other end but to no avail. Eventually, he passed the egg to Piero, who stared at it suspiciously. Glowering at Filippo, he sneered, "You dare present an egg to obtain such a prestigious contract?"

Filippo stepped up, grabbed the egg, and placed it down hard enough to only break the base. Flinging yolk off his fingers, he announced, "Gentlemen, there is your dome."

Giovanni stared at the leaking egg with wonderment and said, "It's so easy! So simple! I can't believe no one ever thought of it before."

"But what will you need?" probed Piero. "Any scaffolding, perhaps?"

The question caught Filippo off guard, but he avoided the trap laid by Piero, asking, "Have you been touched in the head? Do you realize the height of the dome? There are not enough trees in all of Tuscany to come close to building such a structure."

Giovanni turned to Piero. "Yes, Filippo can be abrasive, but from an economic standpoint, he's the only one who will not bankrupt our vaults with lumber alone."

Piero contemplated that, then responded, "If you choose Filippo and he accepts the contract, so be it."

Giovanni nodded his head at Filippo. "Congratulations, you have been awarded the contract."

Others would have broken out into celebratory cheers, but not Filippo. He stood stoically, fully aware that the trials and tribulations ahead would require determination and focus.

Piero crossed his arms. "Let us reconvene in these same quarters tomorrow. I will inform the Wool Merchants' Guild of the panel's judgment." He stared down at Filippo. "As for you, bring back actual plans, not an egg."

The following day, Filippo appeared before the panel as was requested. Under his arm he held the culmination of all his work. After returning the day before, Filippo sequestered himself in his room and reorganized his notes in relation to building a dome for the Santa Maria del Fiore. The countless pieces of paper detailed his plans at almost every level of construction. Filippo laid out his plans on the panel's table but quickly ran out of space. The Medici family walked around examining each drawing. Giovanni smiled, happily content at his work, but Piero rushed into the room.

"I bring news from the Arte della Lana!" shouted Piero, waving a parchment in his hand.

"And? Filippo brought with him much more than an egg," added Lorenzo.

Piero handed Giovanni the parchment, which he quickly scanned. Filippo stepped up to him and asked, "Pray tell me Signore Medici, is my commission still valid?"

"It is still valid. However, the Wool Merchants' Guild feels that with your unproven past, it would reassure them if another appointment was made to help with the construction's burdens," Giovanni told Filippo.

The news infuriated Filippo. "What?!" he yelled. "How dare they question my talent and scope?"

"Calm down, Filippo," suggested Giovanni.

Filippo's respect for Giovanni allowed him to listen to this advice. "I am sorry for the outburst," he apologized. "Can you say who is to split leadership duties with me?"

"It seems the financiers want someone with a proven and trusted history," said a voice long forgotten to Filippo. He turned around to see Lorenzo Ghiberti walk into the room and take a bow. "And that proven and trusted person is me."

Giovanni watched Filippo clench his fist angrily, then advise the young artist, "What will such actions accomplish?"

Filippo stomped his way up to the table, flipped it over, and exited the room without a word.

"Well, at least he didn't break his hand," said Cosimo.

Chapter Sixteen

For over a year, masons had toiled away in blazing furnaces trying to meet the requested order of bricks needed to start the dome. As the necessary supplies were being amassed, Giovanni Medici received a letter late one night in his study. The wax sealing on the paper depicted a sheep and a cross of Christendom, which was the emblem of the Wool Merchants' Guild. Giovanni bit his lip with frustration as his weathered fingers broke the wax. After unfolding the letter and adjusting it to his vision, his eyes meticulously scanned its contents.

Sometime later, Cosimo opened the room's door and saw his father slouched over in a chair staring into the fireplace. "Father, are you well?" asked Cosimo.

"No, my son. I am not well," Giovanni replied, as he kept his gaze fixed on the fire. "*We* are not well. But most importantly, our project is not well."

"How can the project be in jeopardy when it has yet to even start?" Cosimo asked skeptically.

Giovanni held up the letter and spoke, "It would appear our financial partners for finishing Florence's cathedral already have reservations."

"But we conceded to their demands and have allowed Lorenzo Ghiberti to help head the project. What else could they want?" asked Cosimo.

"The Wool Merchants' Guild still worry their money will build nothing but a financial sinkhole," said Giovanni. "They are adamant that Filippo needs to demonstrate his ability prior to beginning the dome. And you caught me wondering how that can be achieved."

After a brief moment of concentration, Cosimo believed he knew the answer. "Can't we pay him to build something like a chapel?" he asked.

"That was where my mind initially went, but if it were only that easy," said Giovanni. "The money we can have for such projects is already tied up with the dome. Providing the bulk of the financing for another construction will be stretching our resources beyond what our coffers currently have."

"Didn't the late Francesco Datini leave a stipulation with the Silk Guild providing some sort of public work in his will?" asked Cosimo.

Giovanni's face broke out into a wide smile as he turned to Cosimo and said, "That's my boy!"

The next day, Giovanni sent word for Filippo to come meet him that evening. As expected, Filippo came exactly when Giovanni wanted, but he hoped that Filippo's obedience would continue during their meeting.

"Would you care for any wine?" asked Giovanni.

"Yes, thank you," answered Filippo. "My throat is somewhat parched from the walk over here."

Giovanni held a crystal decanter of wine in front of the fireplace. The light from the flames made the wine turn a dark pink as the liquid was poured out of the decanter into the goblet. After handing the goblet to Filippo, Giovanni took his seat to discuss business. "Do you know why I summoned you this evening, Filippo?"

"Because you're plying me with drinks, probably to inform of some horrendous news or something," he answered.

Giovanni laughed briefly and responded, "In a sense, yes, but not as horrendous as it could be. Growing up in Florence, do you remember a merchant named Francesco Datini, who is now dead?"

Filippo swirled the wine in his goblet. "A rich man, correct? I was unaware he had died. You have my deepest sympathies."

Giovanni looked at the letter from the Wool Merchants' Guild, then said, "I did not really know him outside of business formalities. And he died nearly a decade ago."

"Oh," said Filippo.

Giovanni lifted his eyes up from the letter and looked Filippo in the eye. "In his will, he bequeathed a great sum of money to the Silk Guild under the condition it would be used to build something of worth for Florentines."

Filippo quickly understood the import of Giovanni's words and said, "I can see where you are going with this. I would normally jump at such an opportunity, but answering the detailed questions posed by Santa Maria del Fiore fills my every waking moment."

Giovanni let out a deep breath, then glared at Filippo, saying, "My words do not provide an opportunity for you. I speak to you with earnest necessity." He watched the reflection of the flames from the fireplace in his young prodigy's eyes, who he knew was very angry. Exercising utmost caution, he chose his next words so as to not further stoke the fires within Filippo: "It is not by my doing, for I already know you are more than capable; however, the Wool Merchants' Guild still has its reservations."

"They've already forced that talentless boil at the project's helm. Is that not enough?" yelled Filippo.

"It would appear not," said Giovanni, as he stood up from his chair and turned around to gaze upon the blaze in the fireplace. "Pay heed to my words and follow them exactly as I tell you. Upon leaving here, you will postpone anything to do with the dome and you will concentrate solely on designing something to honor Datini's last request."

Through gritted teeth, Filippo replied, "He's dead. How can I honor a man I never knew and know nothing about?"

Giovanni turned to Filippo with his arms crossed and said, "Datini was brought up an orphan, so you will be designing an orphanage. If you are to win over the contract from the Silk Guild, you must play to that particular audience. I will do what I can on my end to facilitate the matter and ensure you obtain the contract."

"Why should my talents be wasted upon the abandoned and unwanted by way of an orphanage?" asked Filippo in a stern voice. "I want all of Florence to see my creations, not simply those discarding infants like trash."

Giovanni fumed at Filippo's intolerance. "Unlike the other project, you will have full creative freedom to design anything, as long as it impresses. For failure to impress means you will be discarded from finishing the cathedral."

"Do you not think my talents can impress?"

Giovanni grinned and answered, "Now, here is your chance. If you can, that is."

Biting his lip in frustration, Filippo picked up his glass of wine and tossed its contents into Giovanni's face. Giovanni wiped the wine from his face with a smile as Filippo raged out of the room.

As Giovanni stated, Filippo successfully won the bid from the Silk Guild to honor Datini through his designs for the *Ospedale degli Innocenti*, or Hospital of the Innocents. The idea came to him from the biblical story about the Massacre of the Innocents. Upon hearing from the Magi that the Messiah was to be born, King Herod, the King of the Jews, backed by the Roman Empire, ordered all boys to be killed to maintain his power. Filippo found commonalities between those lost in the biblical infanticide and Florentine orphans and wanted to show Florence's commitment to child welfare through his innovative design.

Having to share creative control with no one, Filippo carefully developed a design utilizing geometric combinations of circles and squares in conjunction with other cultural influences. By aligning a colonnade, Corinthian columns functioned as more than mere decoration, as he deliberately spaced the columns equal to their height, allowing sunlight into the orphanage's loggia, the open arcade. Between the columns, massive arches helped connect each column to the next and provided structural support for the weight above, something not seen in Italy for centuries.

Knowing his time on that particular project was limited, Filippo made the conscious decision to optimize space through large, defined, open courtyards. The overall result left people breathless and epitomized Filippo's understanding of the classical orders of architecture.

Chapter Seventeen

With the critics silenced for the time being, Filippo found himself hurrying through the streets of Florence on an early August morning. Beneath his arm he carried a few rolls of parchment. Despite his unyielding resistance, the Council had successfully forced him to reveal more of his plans, although he had deliberately withheld as much as he could for fear that his opponents might steal his grand design. Each scroll contained notes in a hybrid of Latin, Greek, and Arabic along with various equations. In order to understand each piece, Filippo needed to personally decipher the information.

The unfinished cathedral dominated the skyline like a mountain. Down below, Filippo admired the imposing site for a brief moment, then his imagination took over. He envisioned the dome's construction brick by brick. The completed vision stole his breath and he stood enthralled until a runaway donkey nearly hit him and broke his concentration.

"Hey! *Idiota*! I was standing there!" shouted Filippo.

The donkey's owner ran after the beast waving a crop in the air and yelled, "Get back here, *asino*!"

Filippo continued on his way and soon arrived at the Santa Maria del Fiore, where masons, builders, and manual laborers waited for their instructions. But the throng of workers parted and revealed Lorenzo with members of the *podesta*, the Florentine police force. Lorenzo pointed toward Filippo, saying, "There he is. Arrest him!"

The *podesta* grabbed Filippo, who shouted at the top of his lungs, "What is the meaning of this?" He struggled with all his strength to break free but failed to impede the hired brutes. He relented and started upward to the lackluster structures that swallowed any trace of the Santa Maria del Fiore.

Somewhere beneath the Palace of the People, Filippo was unsure how long he had been isolated in that cramped, damp cell. He felt claustrophobic. The stress of feeling crushed made each passing minute feel like hours. By closing his eyes and focusing on his breathing, Filippo forced himself into a semi-relaxed state. While sitting in the darkness, he remembered that the guards had let him keep his scrolls and that he had a piece of charcoal in his shoes. He placed his blueprints on the floor's uneven stones and did his best to work in the dim light.

"At least you maintained your dignity in this defeat," said Giovanni approvingly.

Filippo glowered up at him and said with all the control he could muster, "Giovanni, please get me out, for I have a dome to build."

Giovanni nodded at the guards, who unlocked the cell. Filippo rolled up the papers, saying, "It was Ghiberti who did this. I shall have my vengeance."

"It was actually *you* who did this," Giovanni said.

The words shocked Filippo. "Absurd! How?" he demanded.

"Remember when you ran off to Rome? Well, you also ran out on some unpaid guild dues. The time away further aggravated the crime, and you became wanted as a debtor," explained Giovanni.

Filippo reddened with embarrassment. "I sincerely apologize for my own stupidity. How much is past due?" he asked.

Giovanni smiled and helped Filippo up to his feet. "The fees have been paid. But I contemplated upon the matter and found the occurrence unusual. While you were building the orphanage, your presence was known; yet, for some reason, they conveniently remembered your debts and chose only then to reclaim them on the first day of construction. Just promise me you will not respond in kind to Lorenzo's spiteful behavior."

Walking out of the cell, Filippo answered, "I let my work speak for myself."

Once outside, Lorenzo tried to organize the towering stacks of bricks that needed to be transported to the top of Santa Maria del Fiore. Unbeknownst to him, another delivery of over a thousand beams of fir trees arrived and needed to be transported up to the roof too. Soon, well over a thousand carts filled with stones pulled up. Meanwhile, in the space not filled with building supplies, crowds of vendors, pedestrians, and onlookers gathered but quickly found themselves trapped in an ever-increasing maze of construction materials.

"Please settle down now," Lorenzo begged the growing mob. "We all must accommodate the burdens of construction."

On the fringe of the mob, Filippo sat atop a pile of lumber watching Lorenzo drown in the disarray. Although he wanted to laugh until his stomach hurt, he knew Lorenzo's lack of understanding would complicate construction, if not slowly ruin the entire project. When the crowd started to voice their displeasure by pelting Lorenzo with rotten fruit and vegetables, Filippo stood up and made his presence known.

A putrefied tomato hit Lorenzo in the chest and splattered all over him. He stared down in disgust at the dripping red spot and scanned the crowd with revenge in his eyes. "I will hang all of you for this!" he vowed.

His words sparked more pelting until Filippo stepped into the line of fire beside Lorenzo and calmed the crowd by raising his hands. "Friends of Florence! Several unforeseen facts came to light today. We apologize for the inconvenience. But we will have the supplies lifted from here shortly." The mob accepted the excuse and dispersed, grumbling.

"It's the damn oxen!" blamed Lorenzo. "Once we get a load delivered to the roof, it takes far too much time to unhitch the beasts from the hoists and set them up again in the opposite direction to simply reverse direction. At this rate, we might have the supplies up there in five or six decades. What are we going to do?"

"We?" responded Filippo. "You mean me."

That night Filippo found himself alone in his room, bent over his desk, working on solving the riddle of the hoist. He dissected the entire machine on parchment but failed to come to a logical solution. Unhitching a stubborn beast like an ox proved to be time consuming. He only knew that the answer must somehow involve keeping the oxen circling in the same direction. He slammed his fist down on the table in yet another display of frustration, crumpled up the paper, and threw it over his shoulder, where it joined countless other paper balls.

The door to his room creaked open, revealing his sister, Cassandra, standing in the doorway. She said, "Mother wanted to know if you felt like joining us for dinner."

Filippo turned to her and said, "I don't have time for useless distractions like food. I must figure out how to bring efficiency to a hoist before the morning. Now, could you please close the door and leave me to my future failure?"

Cassandra walked off but left his door wide open. Filippo stood up and griped, "I swear I have to do everything myself if it is to be done right!"

After slamming the door shut, he slid the sliding lock into place. He repeated the action over and over while studying it, then he had an epiphany. He realized, "This is it! There must be a mechanism or gear to change direction exactly like this." In rapid succession, he continued sliding the lock back and forth, then hurried back to his table to scribble down an idea.

Chapter Eighteen

"It should work now," proclaimed Filippo, "at least, in theory." The workers around him each took a long step back. Filippo tugged the ropes hard to secure a bundle of fir beams, then slapped the oxen on their rears. They bellowed out tremendous grunts and moseyed forward in their wooden circles of confinement. The fir beams rose above the heads of the worried workers. Only Filippo stood proudly below in the shadow, confident of his contraption. A powerful gust of wind sent the beams swaying, causing some in the crowd to flee screaming. As the hoist reached the top, some two hundred feet high, the oxen came to a stop. Filippo stepped up, took a deep breath, and manually slid a metal gear. Confident, he slapped the oxen to continue and soon the bundle of fir beams descended below at a controlled pace accompanied by thunderous applause.

Filippo bowed his head to acknowledge the adulation of the crowd. Meanwhile, Lorenzo held his hands up in victory to accept the praise for his own. Filippo stepped up and hushed the crowd. "Why are you celebrating as if the Rapture is happening? I redesigned the hoist so that we may get back on schedule. Now let us continue, for we have a dome to build."

Later that day, the labyrinth of stone and timber remained untouched on the ground. "Why are all these supplies still down here?" demanded Filippo.

A worker turned to him and explained, "A bottleneck formed up above. The workers could not handle the speed at which everything was going up."

Filippo stepped up on a bundle of timber and said, "Send me up so that I may see for myself."

As the oxen walked in a circle, Filippo rose up to the roof. While being lifted, he took in the majesty of Florence. The sight reminded him of his duty to his city, where his work would be the focal point of all those looking up. If he failed, he would let not just himself down but all those in the city as well.

Filippo stepped off the timber onto the roof carefully, then scrutinized the construction on the Santa Maria del Fiore. Workers formed a single line that stretched across the open diameter and they passed bricks one by one. Filippo's mind assessed the scene and he quickly realized the occupied space was severely limited. In an attempt to solve this riddle, he approached the ledge and gazed into the vast open space below. Many standing where he stood would be wary of the ledge and the open space; at such a height, any fall would be fatal. Despite recognizing the obvious hazard, Filippo concluded that the open space would be the best answer.

A slight breeze brought Filippo back to the present. To his surprise, construction came to a halt and all the workers were staring at him questioningly. One worker stepped forward and said, "Forgive me, Signore Brunelleschi, but please be wary of the ledge."

Teetering on the edge, Filippo pivoted around on his heels in full control and responded, "But if I fear it, how will I be able to harness it? Fear always makes the wolf look bigger." He looked the worker up and down, then asked, "What is your name?"

The man responded, "Rodolfo."

"Pray tell me, Rodolfo, if I am able to free the majority of your men from the rigorous and repetitive task of moving brick by brick, would you be able to build? Not just move supplies from here to there, but really build?"

"Yes, of course, Signore," answered Rodolfo.

The following day, workers did not flood the construction site, nor were oxen using their power to hoist supplies up to the heavens. On this day in early September, most of Florence prepared for the *Festa della Rificolona* that evening, when the children would parade around with paper lanterns. During the day people from the surrounding areas would bring an assortment of goods and wares to sell before the change of seasons. The festival always caused the population of Florence to swell beyond belief, which Filippo knew would only agitate him and provide unneeded stress. To circumvent any potential migraines caused by lost out-of-towners stumbling about and crowding the Florentine streets, Filippo and his little brother, Modesto, made plans to leave the city early that morning.

Somewhere along a curving bank of the Arno River, Filippo struggled to cast a fishing line. He tried using an overhead release but the line got stuck in a bush behind him. Next, he tried a sidearm release but accidentally threw his fishing rod into the river's tide. "How in all things holy do you do this, Modesto?" asked Filippo, bemused.

Further down the bank, Modesto cast his line with his shoulder, then snapped his wrist down at the end. The added motion created additional lag and sent the feathered lure even further out in the river. Filippo watched amazed as Modesto's line went from slack in the flowing current to taut and zigzagging through the water. Modesto carefully managed the length of fishing line while sporadically pulling back to determine resistance. An enormous striped catfish breached the river's surface, fighting against Modesto, then splashed back into the water. Without warning, the line snapped and sent Modesto falling backward on the ground.

Filippo howled with laughter. Modesto stared at the river stony faced and said, "That fish was as good as on our dinner plates."

"The one that just sent you into the dirt?" smirked Filippo.

Modesto reattached a lure to his line, then threaded it through his fishing pole. In another graceful cast, he launched the lure out even further than before. Something quickly snagged on it, and Modesto yanked a small carp out of the water onto the shore. "I don't think that could even fill a bread plate, let alone multiple dinner plates," said Filippo, mocking him.

"At least I caught something aside from a bush, dear brother," retorted Modesto.

Filippo responded, "The last time I went fishing, I was probably eight or nine. Father took me."

Modesto rethreaded his fishing pole and said, "Well, he took me almost every weekend when you ran away to Rome."

Filippo reacted by turning to watch a heron land in the shallows of the Arno, then asked, "Did he ever ask about me?"

"All the time at first. He thought you would return eventually. But his hope waned as time went by. When your name was mentioned, he would become sad. I believe he was regretful about what could have been rather than disappointed."

Filippo stared up at the sky and smiled. Modesto cast out another lure and continued, "Father did always belittle the Baptistery's panels, or at least those that Lorenzo finished."

"If only he could see me now, actually finishing the Santa Maria del Fiore."

Modesto watched his line dance in the current and said, "If it is any comfort, the entire city is already talking about the greatness of your innovative hoist design."

"That specific problem has been solved. Right now, I must contend with transporting the supplies to the top of the cathedral. The workers toil relentlessly but get very little done. If we continue at this pace, the dome might be finished some five or six generations in the future."

"Have you devised any ingenious solutions like your reverse switch gear?" asked Modesto.

Filippo drew a circle connected to a rectangle in the sand and explained, "All I know is, to optimize construction the open space of the cathedral must be used, but most of the workers are scared of plummeting to their death."

"As would be the normal response for most men," added Modesto, when the line jerked him forward. The same enormous striped catfish jumped out of the river. Modesto wrapped the fishing line around his hand and declared, "This time, fish, you will not win."

Each time the fish breached the water, Modesto reeled it in ever so slightly. For over half an hour, Modesto carefully paced his line in an attempt to tire out his catch. He eventually sensed that the fish was tired, so he pulled in his line. Filippo analyzed Modesto's movement in the valiant tug of war against the catfish and understood the engineering principles on display before him. Only a mere arm's length away from Modesto, the catfish summoned its remaining strength and snapped the line.

Modesto kicked the river's tide in anger as Filippo ran up to him and hugged him. "Thank you, dear brother!" he said.

"What are you babbling about? I lost the damn fish," grumbled Modesto. "You don't fish, but the whole point of it is to *catch* the damn fish."

"You are correct, I do not fish. But watching that catfish best you repeatedly struck me with inspiration," asserted Filippo.

"Well, I'm glad one of us got something out of that."

"No, Modesto, it will not just be a single person. All of Florence will benefit."

Chapter Nineteen

Atop the Santa Maria del Fiore, Filippo extended his finger and traced a pulley's rope up on an upright wooden board as it took a ninety-degree turn and connected to perpendicular boards. He had imagined the abstract machine days before and once he was satisfied with the design he asked Rodolfo to assemble a small crew of trusted builders. His faith had not been misplaced because now he stood in front of the actual structure that he had conceived.

Rodolfo rechecked the tightness of each bolt as Lorenzo waited impatiently and grumbled, "Is that damn thing ready yet?"

Filippo smiled back at Lorenzo. "Funny, I heard a group of nuns outside the Baptistery say the same thing regarding the doors."

The insult irked Lorenzo. "I'd probably be done if my presence were not constantly needed here."

"And what is it you're doing again?" inquired Filippo.

As Lorenzo thought of a suitable comeback, a worker stepped off the hoist and hurried over. "Signore Brunelleschi! You have visitors below; it is Signore Medici and others," he said.

The news came as a pleasant surprise to Filippo. "I must go attend to them. In my absence, do not attempt a trial run."

Rodolfo understood. "Yes, Signore," he said.

After a short ride down the hoist, Filippo greeted Giovanni and Cosimo with open arms, asking, "How are Florence's favorite patrons doing on such a lovely day?"

Meanwhile, Lorenzo stared down from the roof contemptuously, then turned to the workers and said, "Prepare the blasted contraption."

Rodolfo reminded him, "Signore Brunelleschi gave us explicit instructions to do otherwise."

Lorenzo yelled, "Do not question me! We're far too behind with construction to dilly-dally around! I will have you kicked off this project for such a lack of respect."

"Yes, Signore," relented Rodolfo, as he led the other workers in strapping a bundle of timber.

On the ground, Cosimo examined the innovation of the reverse gear while Giovanni patted Filippo on the shoulder and said, "Your mind is as creative as that of an artist and as innovative as that of an engineer. Where most men would have succumbed to defeat, you created an answer."

Filippo accepted the compliment proudly; although he knew of his greatness, it was always delightful to have others acknowledge it. Continuing the tour, all three entered the cathedral's massive interior and looked up at the sun shining above. Standing in a pool of light, Filippo spoke confidently, "Take in this sight, gentlemen, for when I am done, it will be no more."

Cosimo tilted his head back. "What's up there? Is that a moving bridge?" he asked.

High on the ledge above their heads, ropes held a bundle of swaying timbers. The sight made Filippo worry, and he ushered Giovanni and Cosimo beneath the cathedral's ceiling, saying, "Excuse me, it appears there is a situation I must address. And we all should leave. *Immediately.*"

Filippo pushed the Medicis to the door hurriedly as a worker yelled out from above, "Watch out!" They turned to the spot where they previously stood to see the bundle of wood crash to the floor. Clouds of dust rose up from the impact and blanketed everything nearby.

Giovanni pointed at the timbers. "Was that your problem?"

The broken wooden beams stacked in the cathedral were beyond mere setbacks. Accidents happen, but this was no accident. Filippo knew someone had blatantly disobeyed him the moment the crane was operated. He thought of what would have happened if he had not seen the timbers in time.

Cosimo wiped the dust off his tunic and gave thanks. "Such a holy place was about to become our grave, if not for your quick action, Filippo."

Outside, Filippo turned to the Medicis and said, "I'll be right back." He stepped on a pallet of bricks and rode it up to the roof, leaving the Medicis below. Upon reaching the top, Filippo yelled, "Which one of you gave the order to start my creation? Whoever it is, you worthless swine should be hanged for attempted murder!"

He glimpsed Rodolfo in the crowd of workers and asked, "Who gave the order? I demand to know."

Rodolfo avoided eye contact and sheepishly replied, "The command came from Signore Ghiberti."

That answer infuriated Filippo. Through gritted teeth, he growled, "Where is he?"

The workers parted to reveal Lorenzo taking inventory of supplies on the far end of the cathedral's roof. In a rage, Filippo stomped across the roof to him. With a quivering finger, he grunted, "You!"

Lorenzo briefly lifted his head up, then refocused on the inventory list and spoke in a condescending tone, "I hate to be the bearer of bad news, but your wooden gizmo gadget failed to work."

Filippo snatched the ledger out of Lorenzo's hand and ripped it in half, screaming, "Your stupidity almost killed the Medicis! You should hope they do not throw you into a cell for attempted murder! I gave strict commands not to commence any trial run in my absence! But no! The great Lorenzo does not have to comply!"

"Do not place any blame on me for that rickety wooden-rope-box your incompetence developed. If you had designed a good model, perhaps we would not be here," retorted Lorenzo.

Filippo slapped Lorenzo in front of the workers gathering around them and said, "Never insult my creations. This one works, like they all do. To appreciate that, you must have some basic intelligence, which you clearly lack."

"It works?" asked Lorenzo. "Then show me. I implore you to show not just me, but all these fine workers."

Filippo turned his back on him and said, "Shut up and follow me. I want to display your stupidity to all those in attendance."

Before leading everyone to the machine, Filippo walked over to the side and motioned for Giovanni and Cosimo to join him on the roof. As they ascended the hoist, Filippo looked back at the workers and said, "I want all of you to remember this day. Lorenzo will surely come down with a case of convenient amnesia and erase this day from his memory. It will be vital that we all remind him so that he learns to be humble." When Giovanni and Cosimo stepped off the hoist, Filippo called for them, "Please come meet the *idiota* who nearly killed two members of Florence's favorite family."

Stepping nose-to-nose with him, Lorenzo invaded Filippo's personal space. "How dare you attack my character?"

"I'm not attacking your character," he explained, "but I will just be proving you wrong. It is that simple, nothing more. Now watch."

Filippo rethreaded the rope through pulleys on the machine and closed the metal latch to secure the rope in place. "Rodolfo, you and your men help bring a load of bricks over here and make sure everything is connected."

Rodolfo nodded and helped his men stack a small pyramid of bricks onto a wooden board. Meanwhile, Filippo commented, "As everyone knows, bricks are heavy and it takes great strength to move them. Coupled with the narrow space allotted to us around the perimeter, transferring bricks becomes quite difficult, which is why I created this contraption. I call it the *castello* and it will eliminate the manual labor required to transport supplies."

He fastened a rope around the wooden base and gave the signal. The bricks rose off the ground up in the air with the aid of a counterweight.

Lorenzo appeared less than impressed. "Congratulations, you reinvented your hoist," he said.

Filippo simply smiled in response to this insult. "Anyone can see that hoist is confined to a vertical path. It goes up and down and nowhere else. To get the supplies positioned as efficiently as possible, I devised a system that goes not just up and down, but in every other direction possible too." His hands spun multiple wooden handles, which adjusted the horizontal length and position of the load. He explained, "My machine is able to take a weighted load far beyond what a single man can lift and place it precisely anywhere I choose, within reason, of course." He gently placed the load of bricks on a ledge. Filippo flashed a smile at Lorenzo, but Lorenzo was not there; instead, he had descended via the hoist to escape embarrassment.

As the workdays waxed into weeks, the genius of Filippo's *castello* was put on display every day. Without it, the workers knew it would take a herculean effort to transport the supplies, all while balancing hundreds of feet above certain death. His engineering solution mitigated their worries only partially because it only took a glance over the edge to instill that fear back into them.

A mason's young apprentice, no older than his early teenage years, wrapped his arms around a bucket of mortar, used his entire body to lift the heavy substance, and struggled to walk with the bucket across the roof. His body swayed from side to side in an attempt to counterbalance it. Nearing the ledge, a rope snagged his foot and sent the boy stumbling toward the edge. The entire incident happened so fast that the boy failed to register any fear; before he knew it, he was staring down into the cathedral's interior. When the boy realized that something was not right, a force pulled him back to solid ground. "Watch your step," said Lorenzo, patting the boy on the head.

The boy looked at Lorenzo's face and hugged him. "Thank you, Signore Lorenzo! You saved my life!"

"And I'm sure you'd do the same for me," he replied, as the workers on the roof gathered around to applaud Lorenzo's quick action.

Rodolfo stepped through the crowd. "Giorgio, what happened?" he asked.

Giorgio turned to Rodolfo, "Master, I would have died if not for Signore Lorenzo."

"A fallen brick tripped up your apprentice and nearly sent him below. But don't fret, while I am here, I will have the best interests for all of you at heart," explained Lorenzo.

Rodolfo replied skeptically. "Our best interests?" he asked.

Chapter Twenty

FLORENCE, 1429

One fairly uneventful afternoon, Filippo peered up at the dome from the ground while comparing it with a hand-drawn parchment for comparison. Over the previous years, a visible red ring had sprouted up on the Santa Maria del Fiore. Brick by brick, Filippo's vision was taking shape right before his very eyes. But his concentration broke when a familiar voice called out from behind, "I pray each day that you know what you're doing and that your work won't turn out to be an eyesore on the face of Florence."

Filippo turned around to find Donatello scrutinizing the miniature dome. Donatello greeted him with a broad smile and a vigorous hug. "Seeing you, old friend, is a welcome sight," he said warmly.

That night in a nearly empty Florentine tavern, Donatello warned Filippo, "Your brick hill better not collapse."

"You have no reason to fret. Nothing I build collapses," said Filippo, sipping on his goblet of wine.

Donatello patted Filippo on the back. "That's what I want to hear. With my sculpture going below, I don't want any bricks raining down upon it."

"What does your piece depict?" asked Filippo.

Donatello lifted his hand up to his mouth and mumbled something incoherently.

Filippo leaned an ear toward him. "Speak up, I can't hear you."

Donatello removed his hand and said, "Abraham and Isaac."

"Copying my old works, I see," remarked Filippo.

"Firstly, it's a good story," explained Donatello. "I'm not a big fan of children, so I approve of anything that encourages child sacrifice. I also remembered that the Medicis seemed to like your panel from years ago. And it just so happens the same family may provide the financial means to make the work possible. Although I sculpt, I know how to play the game."

Filippo rolled his eyes. "Still playing games?"

"From Siena to Pisa to Rome, I somehow, some way received commissions to turn blocks of stone into art, and now I'm back here in Florence playing games along the entire way. Also, who says I'm not copying Lorenzo? Because he did that one as well, if my memory recalls correctly."

Filippo warned Donatello, "Do not try me regarding that scoundrel, let alone mention him when it is not warranted. His sole intent has been to wreck and destroy my project every chance he gets."

Donatello changed the subject by holding up his chalice. "To us, you and me, as here we are today, finally achieving our dreams."

Filippo reluctantly toasted too, saying, "I suppose, but my dream can often be misconstrued for a nightmare from which I am frantically trying to wake up."

"I'm glad I'm not the only one who feels that way," admitted Donatello. "And though it's been quite some time, I want you to know you have my deepest sympathies over your father's passing."

Filippo accepted the condolences with a slight nod of his head. "While we're addressing reflections from the past, I must acknowledge the disrespect and ungraciousness I showed you by leaving Rome so hastily."

Donatello held his empty goblet upside down. "If you get the next round, and the one after that, I'll accept your apology."

Filippo lifted his hand and snapped his fingers at the barkeep, then asked Donatello, "Did my departure bring on any unwarranted hardships?"

"Hardships?" Donatello fought the urge to burst out laughing. "Remember Cardinal Colonna? He concluded that stress coupled with your genius made you go mad, and he did not want the same to happen to me. To alleviate that painful stress, he allowed me to pursue any interest, and his coffers financed it all. Meeting the Cardinal's collection of friends did not hurt either. Currently, I have ongoing projects in Pisa and Siena."

Filippo refilled Donatello's glass from a fresh bottle of wine. "Have you been based in Rome all this time?"

"I actually returned here shortly after your departure. I thought I was the prodigal son returning with enough gold coins to cover any and all of my father's debts. Cardinal Colonna also helped me acquire personalized indulgences written by the Pope absolving my whole family of any potential sin. I was a son who left as an abject failure, but in my mind I would return having achieved the success my father always strove for day in and day out.

"I departed Rome one morning led by those hopeful visions and found myself outside the southern gates sometime late that night. The gates were closed but a handful of coins to the guards gained me entry. I quickly arrived at my home. Through the windows I saw only darkness; the door was locked, but the spare key remained where I had left it. Upon entering, I found myself in a drafty, empty abode. I saw the dining table at which I had eaten so many meals as a child. Fresh ashes had been swept away from the hearth, reassuring me that someone still lived there. I lit a nearby candle and sat down at the table waiting for my father to return.

"At some point, weariness overcame my body and I fell asleep at the table. But my dreams were broken by my father's voice waking me like a hammer to the head. I awoke to find him guzzling a bottle of wine. It seemed that time had not lessened his opinion of me running up that bar tab. His guild had set out to make an example out of him and so he could not find work anymore; it was as if he were a leper. Eventually, the only gainful employment he could obtain was that of an undertaker.

"As he placed a dirt-covered shovel against the wall, he yelled at me to wake up, demanding to know what I was doing breaking into his house. I withstood his verbal abuse, reached into a satchel, and presented him with a handful of the gold. I told him it was his. He snatched the satchel to examine the gold himself, after which I revealed a stack of indulgences. Oh, the indulgences really intrigued him. For a brief moment, I actually thought he saw my remorse for all my youthful follies, but soon he started ripping the gifts to shreds.

"He was not yelling but calmly told me that I was a gullible, talentless lout responsible for ruining his life. Yet, during the insults he found a way to further rub salt into the festering wounds he had reopened. Each insult was accompanied by a single coin pelted at me, one after the other. This was not what

I had returned for, so I stood up in silence wanting to leave. But with a wine bottle in hand, he kept preventing my departure by stepping in front of me and blocking my path. He finished the wine, then he attacked.

"I lunged for the door, but he broke the empty bottle on my face. I fell into the wall and came back to my senses with him on top of me trying to stab me with the remaining shards of the wine bottle still grasped in his hand. Fending off his assault the best I could, I frantically flailed around until I found the shovel. I thrust the bladed edge into the soft flesh on the side of his neck. Dark crimson blood gushed everywhere. He was gasping and clutching his throat when I stood up to leave. I walked and never turned back. I even waited for quite some time before I showed my face in this city after that. However, it turns out no one cared he was dead. I still don't know how I feel about that. But here I am, still breathing."

Filippo held up his glass. "And, old friend, here we are, just like old times."

Meanwhile, a messenger hurried into the tavern and scanned the few patrons present. "That man looks very familiar. Where have I seen him before, Filippo?" asked Donatello.

Filippo glanced over his shoulder and recognized the messenger. "That's one of Giovanni's couriers."

Upon seeing Filippo, the messenger made his way to him and spoke solemnly, "Signore Brunelleschi, with a painful heart, I come to inform you that Giovanni di Medici no longer resides within our earthly realm."

Chapter Twenty-One

FLORENCE, 1429

Outside the Medici residence workers placed their chisels on the mortar between the stones that formed a wall. As their hammers hit the chisels, the mortar broke away. At first, their labor exposed only a sliver of the luxurious interior, but as the day progressed, the slit enlarged until the entire wall was dismantled.

Meanwhile, inside the residence Cosimo knocked on a door. "Lorenzo, it is time," he said. Hearing no response, Cosimo opened the door, leaned his head into the room, and saw his younger brother slumped over on the edge of his canopy bed. Lorenzo turned to his older brother and wiped tears away from his eyes. "Do you need a moment, brother?" asked Cosimo.

Lorenzo looked at him with sullen eyes and released a deep breath from his shuddering body. Cosimo approached him, placed a comforting hand on his shoulder, and said, "Come. We must be strong for Mother. And besides, what would Father think? He never approved of grown men crying."

A subtle smile appeared on Lorenzo's face as he responded, "You are correct. Let us do what we need to and get it over with. It is what Father would want."

Cosimo led Lorenzo out of the ornate bedroom into the hallway. They journeyed down the hallway with somber steps until they reached a double door. Cosimo gripped the handle and pushed it open. Turning back to his brother, he realized how sad Lorenzo was and comforted him. "Sons bury fathers, as it should be. And do not think you are alone, because you are not. He was my father too."

Inside the master suite Giovanni's pale body was placed on a table. His sons approached it, steeling themselves for what they were about to see. Cosimo removed multiple gold rings from his father's fingers and placed them on another table. The two brothers disrobed the body and washed it with tender care. Then they dried and dressed their father and sprayed perfume on him. With their duty as sons fulfilled, they walked out of the room, but Lorenzo spotted Giovanni's rings on the table and said, "Cosimo, do not forget your rings."

A short time later, workers had transported Giovanni's body from his bedroom to a parlor on the ground floor. In the back of the room, a woman wearing all black watched the scene unfold, then removed her veil. Giovanni's widow, Piccardi, approached her husband's body. When they first met years ago, her father had been appalled at her choice of suitors. Their family, the Bueris, had been held in the highest regard for countless generations; however, Piccardi wanted to marry an unproven man from a common family with only banking aspirations. In her youth, poets traveled from distant lands to sing praises of Piccardi's beauty. Many believed her to be the reincarnation of Helen of Troy, but now here she was interested in a Giovanni, who looked like a dwarfed ape and had misaligned, bulging eyes. Despite his flaws, Giovanni's persistence and intelligence would ultimately win Piccardi over. After nearly forty years of a wonderful marriage, she knew she had chosen correctly and could not imagine traveling through life with anyone else at her side. With tears in her eyes, she leaned over and kissed her lover one last time, until they would be reunited again in heaven.

Filippo and Donatello watched as workers removed Giovanni's body through the hole in the exterior wall, which was done to prevent the departed's soul from returning to the house. Because of their close relationship with Giovanni, Filippo and Donatello joined the family for the funeral procession through the streets and this melancholic stroll made them all reflect for a moment on their own mortality. However, Piccardi wanted not just all of Florence to grieve and commemorate her late husband, she wanted the residents of all the surrounding Tuscan provinces to do so too. To accomplish this feat, she had hired professional mourners who all wailed, howled, and screeched to an obnoxious degree. Donatello confided to Filippo, "When I go, please do not honor my greatness by sending me off with an annoying chorus of raucous cats."

When the procession reached the Old Sacristy of the Basilica of San Lorenzo, Filippo silently rejoiced to see the mourners leave. Thankfully, their services were no longer required and Filippo's ears did not have to suffer any further. But when the priests unlatched the church doors, a wave of nauseating fumes seeped out. Both Filippo and Donatello fought the urge to vomit, especially once they saw multiple dead bodies in various states of decay.

When workers placed Giovanni's body into a marble sarcophagus, Filippo knew he only had to breathe through his mouth a little longer. At his side, the stench of decomposition had overcome a green-faced Donatello. Filippo whispered, "Do you not remember getting lost in the Cloaca Maxima? That was much worse."

In a hushed voice, a pale, sweaty Donatello replied, "You're not helping my situation."

Shortly later, the workers sealed the sarcophagus and people filed out of the church. Filippo and Donatello hurried to the front to escape the smell, but Cosimo called for them, saying, "Filippo, Donatello, there is something I must tell you two."

Donatello stepped toward the door, but Filippo grabbed his tunic. "He wants us both," he said.

"I don't know how much longer I can last in this box of death," said Donatello.

Filippo reminded him tersely to breathe out of his mouth.

They approached an emotionally distraught Cosimo, who was struggling to maintain his composure. He hugged each of them and stated, "Thank you for coming here today. It means a lot."

Filippo consoled him. "Your father was like a father to each of us. A man that great will surely be missed by all."

"I agree," said Cosimo. "And I believe he should rest in something that reflects his contribution to all those around him more so than just a modest, drab sarcophagus in a nondescript alcove. Would you be interested in assisting me with an endeavor to preserve my father's legacy?"

Filippo smiled. "It would be beyond an honor to assist you, my friend, to recognize the greatness of your father, my late friend, Giovanni."

Cosimo studied Donatello's gaunt face and asked, "Are you all right?"

Donatello shook his head slightly and Filippo spoke for him, saying, "The absence created by your father's passing has really affected Donatello, as it has all of us who knew him." Filippo headed to the door, saying, "It feels as if inspiration has flooded my being with ideas to cherish Giovanni's memory."

"Then please do not let me interfere with divine providence. And thank you again for everything. Father always thought of you two as his sons," said Cosimo. Filippo nodded at the compliment while gently pushing Donatello toward the church doors. Around ten steps away from the exit, Donatello broke into a sprint to get outside, where, finally overwhelmed by the stench, Donatello vomited on the church steps.

In the early evening Filippo took in the view from the top of the Santa Maria del Fiore and unrolled a parchment, saying, "What makes my approach different is that I will utilize two domes, a dome within a dome."

Donatello sipped from a wine bottle and rolled his eyes. "That's your big secret? A dome within a dome?"

"There's more to it," added Filippo. "There will be structural hoops built into the exterior dome for an added brace."

"Two domes and a hoop. You sound like a choir boy describing a nude woman for the first time," jested Donatello. "There is something that my mind has been dwelling upon with Giovanni's passing. Do you think the patronage will change with Cosimo at the helm?"

Filippo contemplated the question. After a moment, he responded, "Giovanni raised Cosimo in such a way that he developed a love of art that grew and blossomed. Unlike many, he understands the creative mind and fickle nature of an artist. I feel he will extend his late father's patronage."

"Let us hope so," agreed Donatello.

As the daylight disappeared, they made their way to the hoist and rode it down, when Donatello asked, "Back in Rome, when the letter of your father's passing arrived, did you ever regret not opening it then and there?"

"Honestly? I have lost many hours of sleep regarding that very same question echoing throughout my head," revealed Filippo. "But it begs a further question, would I be where I am now, fulfilling what he said could never be done? Upon learning of his death, it hit me hard, but it eventually motivated me to get to where I am today."

Donatello added, "Do you ever think that he guided you here?"

"Each and every time I lay my eyes on the dome's construction," said Filippo, as they disembarked from the lowered hoist.

They walked down the street, but Donatello realized that Filippo had stopped a few steps behind him. He asked, "Everything okay, Filippo?"

Filippo clutched his abdomen and said, "It surely does not feel that way." Then he collapsed.

Donatello rushed to his friend's side. "Filippo?! Filippo?!" Searching the nearly empty streets, he yelled, "Help! Someone help!"

Chapter Twenty-Two

FLORENCE, 1430

Filippo awoke on the empty streets of Rome beneath a night sky void of stars, a sky that resembled a suspended dark canvas. No lit hearths could be seen through windows, only fathomless blackness. No snippets of conversation between Romans filled the air; the only ambient sound was a piercing silent stillness. Hurrying down the road, Filippo discovered no sleeping drunkards littering the ground. The streets were clean and immaculate. "Is this Rome?" he asked himself.

He searched for any other soul but found no sign of life. Wandering alone, he called out, "Is anyone there? Anyone at all?"

The silence was disheartening until Filippo caught a glimpse of something or someone clad in dark red fabric standing apart from the gray buildings. But it disappeared around a corner like a wisp of smoke. Filippo pursued it in a mad dash. But upon turning the corner, he laid eyes upon the Pantheon and the twirling cloth-being vanishing within its walls.

As Filippo followed, his eyes strayed to the fountain in front of the Pantheon. Never had he seen a fountain in Rome where water did not flow or splash, yet here was one before him. He cupped his hand and placed it in the pool of water. Even though the temperature outside was pleasant, the water within the fountain was frigid. The bitter cold turned Filippo's hand numb as the water slipped through his fingers. Suddenly, a woman called for him by name: "Filippo." He turned to the Pantheon, and the voice called his name once again: "Filippo."

Filippo ignored the mystery of the fountain and shuffled toward the Pantheon, which had been returned to its ancient grandeur. Beneath the Oculus, Maria stood in the middle with her back turned to him. "Maria?" asked Filippo.

He made his way to her, but she kept turning away. Frustration growing, Filippo tilted his head up to the Oculus, but when he looked back Maria had vanished. He ran out of the Pantheon in search of her, only to discover the surrounding buildings had vanished as well, leaving only eerie darkness.

Filippo reentered the Pantheon, but was now transported to the inside of the Santa Maria del Fiore. Stones slid out of the wall and formed a spiral staircase that allowed him to ascend to the roof. At the top, workers toiled and slaved constructing the dome with great precision. Some workers delivered building supplies, then stepped off the edge, which worried Filippo. He ran to the ledge and grabbed a worker's shirt to prevent him from falling, but the fabric slipped through his fingers and he watched the nameless worker plummet to his death.

Alarmed, he searched for whoever was in charge, when a leather whip hit him across his back and sent him to his knees. As Filippo cowered in pain, Lorenzo revealed himself with the whip in hand, demanding, "Get back to work! My legacy depends on it!"

Firm resolve galvanized within Filippo. Rising to a knee, he sneered back, "You dare address me as a subordinate! This is *my* project!"

Lorenzo cracked the whip at him in response, but Filippo ignored the pain and stood up. The workers stopped construction and watched the defiance unfold. Lorenzo hissed, "Your insolence will serve as an example for the others. My word is the sole authority. My vision is supreme."

"I will not let you steal my dreams," yelled Filippo.

Lorenzo laughed. "You speak the impossible."

Filippo glared at Lorenzo. "No, I build the impossible."

"How can a dead man build?" asked Lorenzo. "A dead man does nothing but die," he added, wrapping the whip tightly around Filippo's throat.

Fearing for his life, Filippo pried his fingers into the constricting leather as his vision began to blur. With darkness descending, all he felt was the cool air blowing through his hair until the sudden impact on the hard marble. Above, Lorenzo peered over the edge and tossed bricks down at Filippo. "You should have listened to your father. It won't be done. It *can't* be done. All your wasted dreams led you through a life of failure and foolery. Be proud your father is not here among us to see what a disappointment you are and will remain, for it would surely kill him a second time."

In the blink of an eye, the bricks and stones forming the Santa Maria del Fiore reassembled into a colossal statue of Lorenzo. As the news spread, the residents of Florence began to flood the streets. Filippo lay on the ground unable to move and the Florentines crowded around, but no one paid him the slightest attention. Instead, each head craned upward to the imposing statue of Lorenzo that loomed over the entire city.

~

"We must apply more leeches," suggested Biagio, a doctor holding up a glass bottle filled with the bloodsuckers. "The poor soul has far too much blood flowing through his veins," he added. "We must drain the excess immediately, or else his condition will only worsen."

Another doctor, Ludovico, shook his head with annoyance at the diagnosis and said, "The ailment is not his blood. It's his teeth. Even a fool knows that. I just need to pull them all out. And maybe strap some special healing roosters to his body for an added measure."

Giuliana looked indignant as she stood over Filippo's bedridden and unconscious body. "Absolutely not," she replied.

Yet another doctor, Vespasiano, proposed, "There might be an alternative remedy. When I was learning the ancient art of healing, my teacher told me of a cure originating in the Far East. Supposedly, when Alexander the Great obtained wounds fatal to all men, this remedy allowed him to live. Augustus used the technique again while on one of his many campaigns."

"Enough. Just do it already," pleaded Giuliana.

Vespasiano revealed a parchment and a quill and said, "All we need him to do is write 'Abracadabra' down eleven times and he will be healed. The secret is going up to eleven. Most stop at ten, but everyone knows eleven is one more than ten, hence it has more healing power."

The supposed cure disappointed everyone in the room. "Why not go to twelve?" asked Ludovico.

"Twelve? Are you mad?!" yelled Vespasiano. "But I would expect that coming from someone wanting to extract all his teeth, as if that would do anything."

Giuliana spoke directly to Vespasiano. "You do know that Filippo is unconscious, so how can he grip a quill to write anything at all?"

"I have an idea," exclaimed Vespasiano. He placed the quill in Filippo's fingers, held it in place, and attempted to scribble the magical word on paper.

Ludovico lifted a bag with quarreling roosters and offered, "I can still attach the chickens to him, if you so desire."

"Don't forget about the perils of excess blood," reminded Biagio, holding up the leeches.

As the doctors attempted to persuade Giuliana, a rooster escaped from Ludovico's bag and fluttered around the room. Everyone concentrated on capturing the rooster, but they all failed to notice Filippo's eyes burst open. After the brief commotion, Ludovico shoved the rooster back into the bag and looked toward the empty bed. "What happened to your son? Where did he go?"

"Ha! My cure worked!" gloated Vespasiano.

Ludovico held up his bag of roosters and argued. "It was the rooster chasing away the evil spirits!"

"Or perhaps it was the magic of my leeches!" said Biagio; now all three doctors confronted the other, each man believing that his cure had worked.

Meanwhile, out in the hall, Filippo painstakingly made his way to the stairs, when Giuliana appeared behind him and demanded, "Just where do you think you're going, Filippo?"

He fell to the ground and dragged himself along the floor. "I must get to work, before all my dreams are lost."

"You have been bedridden with a fever for almost two weeks. You are going nowhere," instructed Giuliana.

"But I must," said Filippo, before he passed out.

A day later Filippo woke up again in his bed. This time the only other person in the room was Giuliana, who was sleeping in a nearby chair. Filippo threw back the sheets and rose from his bed, careful to make as little sound as possible. Through the window, he caught the sun during its morning ascent and exhaled a sigh of relief. Walking to the door, he walked toward his sleeping mother, kissed her on the cheek, and said, "Thank you," then exited his room.

Bounding down the stairs, Filippo showed the exuberance of a young soul, not that of a middle-aged man who had just woken up from a two-week coma. His brother stared up at him in utter disbelief. "Filippo? Is that you or do my eyes deceive me?" asked Modesto.

He smiled and said, "It is me," then he opened the front door.

"I don't think you should be leaving," warned Modesto. "Do you not remember you tried yesterday, only to crumple in a heap in the upstairs hall?"

"If I only made out to the hall yesterday, then today I have done double that by making it this far," declared Filippo. "I have been absent from construction for some time. I must show the workers that I am still here. If Mother awakes and asks about me, please tell her that I will be back shortly. Unless I pass out on the streets, in which case, please make sure to look for me."

Before Modesto could respond, Filippo closed the door behind himself.

Chapter Twenty-Three

FLORENCE, 1430

Outside, Filippo journeyed through the Florentine streets still wearing his nightgown. Passersby gaped, gawked, and snickered, but Filippo did not pay them the slightest attention. With each step, his nightmare flashed vividly in his mind. But upon glimpsing the dome from afar, he exhaled a sigh of relief, for it was still far from finished. Filippo composed himself, realizing that he had worried too much, and with that realization he smiled.

The construction workers on the ground turned their heads, shocked to see Filippo in his night clothes, but they knew better than to heckle him and continued with their daily tasks. Filippo stepped on the hoist and rode it upward.

While he was scrutinizing the construction effort, a voice called out, "Signore Brunelleschi!" Rodolfo made his way over and said, "You are a welcome sight, in sharp contrast to the daily disarray and confusion that prevailed in your absence."

The information snuffed out Filippo's jovial mood and he looked worried. He asked, "Please, my friend, what has been the problem?"

Rodolfo led Filippo over to the construction site to examine a section of the dome that was about thirty feet high. At the base was a sturdy zigzag pattern of bricks that had been Filippo's idea. Supported above was the work Lorenzo had thought of: a thin veil of bricks with unset mortar. The recent work infuriated Filippo, so he asked, "How can this do? It will fall over and collapse the moment a bird flies past it. Where is Lorenzo?"

Workers pointed to Lorenzo at the other end of the roof and Filippo's bare feet pounded down across the top of the Santa Maria del Fiore toward him. A million different scenarios rushed into Filippo's mind. A part of him simply wanted to push Lorenzo over the edge and delight in his descent. If questioned about the death, Filippo's excuse would be that Lorenzo had slipped. If that did not work, surely Filippo's friends in high places would come to his defense and keep him out of prison. Regardless of any potential indictment, he knew the appropriate response he could expect from the city of Florence. Lorenzo would be forever placed on an artistic pedestal and his skills would be exaggerated and his memory would be exalted. But what Filippo feared the most was that his contribution would be erased from history and superseded by that of his nemesis.

While Lorenzo wrote on parchment the inventory of stones, he spotted Filippo approaching. "Glad to see you eluded death's grasp. While your body was contemplating giving up, I took the initiative to alter some of the original design. Nothing to worry about, only small stuff. And nice clothes."

Lorenzo's attitude irritated Filippo, but he fought the urge to push him off the roof and instead responded, "Your stupidity has placed the lives of those below in peril."

"How dare you take that tone with me?" demanded Lorenzo. "My stupidity will make both of us richer than we can imagine, while pleasing our patrons because we will have finished far below the expected budget."

Filippo smacked the parchment from Lorenzo's hands. "We were already under budget! Do you not even understand the potential outcomes of cutting building costs? You have stopped following the plans for the stone masonry support. And where is my second dome? My plans called for a dome within a dome!"

"I thought that was a mistake brought on by your delirious mind. Besides, we are only commissioned for a single dome, not two," pointed out Lorenzo.

"Do you know how to build, you imbecile?" said Filippo accusingly. "These are not some cosmetic features you can simply forgo on a whim if you do not find them pleasing to the eye. They are intricate necessities required to sustain the building. Or else, all of Florence risks the dome toppling over and raining down bricks, stone, and mortar on their heads. Your attempt at cutting corners to line your pockets is pathetic. One hundred years from now, when you and I are both dead and rotting in the ground, will that extra money be of any use?"

The words offended Lorenzo deeply. "Such audacity to insult my intelligence! Everything you have done was made possible through your handlers, the Medici. You are nothing more than a trained lap dog who got lucky and befriended the right owners. Unlike you, I did not come to any of my accolades through conniving and nepotism," he said angrily.

"It appears you conveniently forgot the fiasco your father created years ago when we were vying to finish the doors for the Baptistery," said Filippo slyly.

Shaking his finger at Filippo like a club, Lorenzo scolded him before a growing crowd of workers, saying, "You have always considered everyone to be beneath you. Yet when someone such as myself surpasses you in any and all capacities, you only show disdain and animosity. We stand on holy ground and we are driven by piety to finish our city's beloved cathedral. I find it unimaginable that your stubborn rashness has yet to be replaced by humility, especially after you nearly succumbed to a fatal illness."

Filippo calmed his demeanor and spoke so that all could hear. "I do not know how to bake bread; therefore, you will never see me arguing with a baker. In all my years upon this earth, I have never plowed a field, nor planted seeds, nor even cut down a single tree. And at no time will you ever hear me speak or profess with any knowledge of such. Instead, I have dedicated the majority of my life to understanding buildings from antiquity. Where so many others take them for granted, I desired to learn how such structures had been built. Though time obscured the wisdom of the ancients, I did not let this deter me, and through meticulous study, these secrets revealed themselves to me. What you consider rashness is nothing more than a comprehensive understanding."

"There you go again!" shrilled Lorenzo. "The sheer thought of someone eclipsing your work cannot even penetrate your head! I know it must be painful that I have always bested you at everything and have made you a perennial runner-up in life. It started years ago with me winning the Baptistery contract, and now here it is with me improving your design and making it more cost efficient."

Filippo reminded him, "Your improved design has yet to be proven."

"The only judge for such will be time itself. In a thousand years from now, Florence will gaze up to the heavens, spot my dome, and recognize me, Lorenzo Ghiberti, as the genius who achieved the impossible."

Lorenzo put his hands on his hips and puffed out his chest, then suddenly the ground began to shake. Some on the Santa Maria del Fiore quickly grabbed on to anything. Others lowered their base and said a prayer, but a stronger tremor hit, causing the entire church to sway. After a brief moment of uncertainty, Lorenzo gazed up to see his design still standing upright. He bragged to all, "See, everyone! My work still stands up, even to the Almighty!"

As soon as Lorenzo uttered those words, all of Florence shook with an even more intense quake. The parts of the dome Lorenzo had supervised fell and crashed down onto the roof and into the interior of the cathedral while the lower portion remained sturdy and immovable. When the quake subsided, all the workers craned their heads to look at an embarrassed Lorenzo. He attempted to provide an excuse. "Such acts are not of this world. It was nothing more than a lesson in boasting. Let this be an example for us all to practice modesty. Now, let's get back to work."

The workers did not move; instead, they stood with all eyes focused on Lorenzo. Rodolfo approached Filippo. "Signore Brunelleschi, we will not work with him."

"Be quiet and return to work," ordered Lorenzo.

Filippo berated Lorenzo, saying, "You placed his life and everyone else's lives in peril with your disastrous design. Their complaints are beyond valid."

Ignoring the words the best he could, Lorenzo returned to checking inventory, but workers impeded his path. He stepped to the side, but more workers approached him. "I will not be humiliated like this! Especially by someone like you, Filippo! You ruined it! You sabotaged my wall!"

With workers at his side, Rodolfo appeared in front of Lorenzo and presented him with a choice: "Signore Ghiberti, you may leave this roof on your own accord, or we will help you down."

Defeated for the time being, Lorenzo bit his lip and stomped over to the hoist. When descending, he screamed out for all to hear, "This is not over!"

Chapter Twenty-Four

As Filippo closed the door to his home and stepped out, he was surprised to see how sparsely populated the streets were. Normally, on a Saturday the streets brimmed with Florentines enjoying the pleasant weather. But Filippo was focused on a more important matter. A year before he had been given a contract to design and oversee the construction of another basilica in Florence, Santo Spirito. Whenever Filippo worked on anything pertaining to Santo Spirito, he found himself investing all his energy into the project because his primary commitment was to the completion of the Santa Maria; still, the financial compensation for working on Santo Spirito was too generous to ignore.

With another structure acting as a blank canvas, Filippo had the opportunity to create something without being confined. In his blueprints he sought to capture the basilica's namesake, the Holy Spirit. The initial idea came to him one night as he sat brooding at his desk. Unable to find inspiration of any sort, Filippo gazed out an open window and up to the stars. The sight of the celestial objects created a sense of humility within him, and he closed his eyes and said a prayer. The moment he opened his eyes, a calm wind blew through the window, filling his room with the cool night air. Seconds later, the gentle breeze picked up speed and became a voracious flurry. Filippo watched in awe as the rush of air lifted the papers on his desk and blew them all over the room. He gathered them up from the floor after the wind eventually settled.

Like wind filling the sails of a ship, the wind that night filled Filippo's mind with inspiration and was eventually reflected in the design of Santo Spirito. His plans called for a reliance on curves to symbolize the Holy Spirit, or the "Breath of God." On paper, dome-vaulted columns stretched down the basilica's main aisle. On the ceiling, four shell-shaped apses called tribunes incorporated aspects of Roman architecture. Even the name tribune originated from ancient Rome and referred to an official elected by the plebeians to act on their behalf.

Calcio Fiorentino, or Florence football, originated in 1430, when the Holy Roman Emperor, King Charles V, laid siege to the city of Florence. In a display of toughness and fortitude, Florentine soldiers mocked the soldiers of the Holy Roman Empire by fighting each other. After ten months of laying siege to a city with its citizens beating each other up, King Charles V relinquished the battle and recalled his forces. However, the sentiment within Florence's citizenry did not dissipate and an annual tradition arose to commemorate the event. On that day, neighbors become rivals and venture off to war against their fellow Florentines, all with hopes of bringing honor to their district.

Every year since then, the four quarters of Florence, Santa Croce, San Giovanni, Santa Maria Novella, and Santo Spirito, each send a team consisting of twenty-seven players to participate in the yearly remembrance. Played on a sanded pitch for fifty minutes, each team vies against the other in a massive full-contact fistfight with the purpose being to throw a leather ball into the opponent's goal. Six referees and a line judge are assigned to try to keep order as best they can in a game designed to reflect a military battle. Meanwhile, residents of a particular district flood the surrounding areas to cheer on their team while booing anyone else. When the dust settles, bragging rights and a ceremonial cow go to the winning team.

Many considered the carnage too small to be a war, but too cruel to be a mere game. Filippo felt the game reflected the dual identities of Florence itself. If not for the fierceness of the city's violence and willingness to take up arms in its own defense, artists like him within the city surely would not be able to ply their trade. Rome forged a gladiatorial mentality that was still alive and well in the populace of Florence. Like the buildings or the streets, *Calcio Fiorentino* helped to create an integral and defining part of the city's identity.

While walking south on his way to Santo Spirito, Filippo began to notice more and more people crowding the streets. Upon arriving at the Ponte Vecchio, he heard a great commotion, then eventually saw its source: a mass of Florentines creating an immovable wall of humanity on the southern side of the Arno. The sight upset Filippo, who would have to traverse the throng to get to the building site. Unable to navigate through the crowd, he relinquished his plans of working on the construction site that day and returned to the silent solitude of his desk.

Chapter Twenty-Five

The previous years had been tumultuous for Cosimo di Medici. A rival family, the Pazzis, had imprisoned him in the Palazzo Vecchio. Although many clamored for his head, Cosimo successfully used his family's resources to bribe the appropriate officials and escape the volatility of his beloved Florence. In exile, Cosimo longed to return but was aware of the grave consequences his presence would bring, so he initially bided his time in the city of Padua. Upon arriving there he found himself visiting the city's famous university almost daily. Some days he would sit in on university lectures; on others he spent hours reading in the library.

After the weeks had become months, Cosimo relocated to Venice, where his younger brother, Lorenzo, joined him to wait out his exile. In Venice, the constant presence of flowing water captivated Cosimo. Florence may have the Arno, he thought, but nothing was comparable to the Venetian canals. Of the two cities, he found the aquatic charm of Venice more alluring, even dwelling on the thought of relocating his entire court to Venice. However, the first time he witnessed a drunken Venetian fall off a bridge and land in a canal, he had flashes of his artists drowning after a night of heavy drinking. But within a few years, Cosimo was beckoned by all of Florence to return where great fanfare greeted him, but seeing the nearly completed Santa Maria del Fiore made Cosimo forget all about his warm homecoming.

Atop the roof of the Santa Maria del Fiore, Filippo bounded around the dome and Cosimo hurried to catch up. "When I left our city, you built enough to give the basic idea to any passerby down below. But now that I've returned, I can finally see for myself what all those travelers told me," he said, panting.

Filippo asked, "Why would they be talking about the dome? I have not finished it yet. When I'm done, then they will have something to talk about."

"Anyone who sees your work understands the greatness before them. It is a testament to your perseverance and self-taught genius," said Cosimo.

Filippo added, "No, it is a testament to all of Florence and our resoluteness."

The words warmed Cosimo's heart. "There were times many thought this was far-fetched, but here you are, my friend, within arm's reach of achieving your dream. Under your leadership and guidance, you made the impossible possible. What was once unattainable, you engineered into reality."

Filippo nodded his head to acknowledge the kind remarks, but he wondered how people would receive his masterpiece. It was not just the opinions of his contemporaries that concerned him; he also ached to know what succeeding generations would think of his work. Would his work become a testament to his city's greatness? Would people in the future categorize his work as belonging in the same league as the Pantheon?

"How much longer do you think will be needed?" asked Cosimo.

Filippo pondered on the question, then replied, "There is still space up top for a lantern or another decorative object. For some reason, I visualize melding aspects from the Colossus of Rhodes with those from the Lighthouse of Alexandria."

Cosimo's imagination took off. "I can already see something like a massive gold lantern adorning the top. It will cast out a beacon attracting lost souls to salvation below us in the church."

Filippo walked to the hoist. "Follow me, for I have more to show you."

Inside the Santa Maria del Fiore, Filippo and Cosimo stood below the dome's massive interior. The enormity of it overwhelmed Cosimo, who asked, "How large is that again?"

Filippo pointed to his foot. "If you take the average size of a capable man's foot and use it to form the lengths of a square, the ceiling above is around 38,750 squares."

"And what exactly do you want to do with a space that grand?" asked Cosimo.

Filippo smiled with a glint in his eyes. "I plan to make it reflect the greatness of Florence beneath the Tuscan sun. I want to place the sun above so that it will always shine down upon us."

Cosimo struggled to understand the idea. "So, you will need buckets of yellow paint?" he asked.

Filippo scoffed. "Yellow paint? Florence is much better than yellow paint, and I think you'll agree. We'll leave the yellow paint to the amateurs."

"Then what will you need to make that happen?" inquired Cosimo.

"Looking up, I see the potential grandeur of our beloved city, one that is now more prominent and wealthy than ever. And we need something to demonstrate such," stated Filippo.

"When I close my eyes, I see a dome of gold reflecting the light of God below."

"Gold?" Cosimo choked on the word. "That would be quite a lot of gold, but it might be feasible."

"Wonderful," said Filippo, delighted.

"I said it *might* be feasible," reminded Cosimo. "Did you forget I have sons now? Giovanni's still young, but Piero has earned the nickname 'the Gouty.' Do you know how expensive it is to feed a kid with the nickname 'the Gouty'? A lot, if you were wondering. He tried to ride a pony, and that poor beast will never be the same."

"Did he break the pony's back?" asked Filippo.

"If only, my friend. We tried to lift him onto the pony but to no avail. Piero really wanted to get on it, so in an attempt to keep him quiet we strapped him to a rope and pulley. A group of stout men elevated him, but his weight was more than the rope could take, and it snapped and Piero landed in a pile of horseshit. He cried but I laughed for days and days."

Filippo laughed, as a young messenger entered the church and presented him with an ornate parchment. "Signore Brunelleschi, this message is for you."

"Thank you," said Filippo, accepting the letter. The massive wax seal formed the image of two crossed keys, which symbolized the keys Jesus gave St. Peter. Filippo knew only a single man held the keys to St. Peter and that man was the Pope.

Filippo broke the papal seal and read the contents. "It's from Pope Eugene IV. He wants to consecrate the cathedral in March."

"For Easter or on Florence's New Year?"

Filippo looked up from the paper. "Both. This year, it appears they fall on the same day."

❧

Weeks later, after a tiring day in his workshop, Donatello entered a tavern seeking the inspiration of his muse in the form of wine. "Barkeep, I am in dire need of subsistence. I worked all day and now I fear sobriety is complicating my judgment. Do you have any possible remedies for my brain?"

The barkeep nodded. "I have just the remedy, a red from Veneto."

"Wonderful. Where is it?" asked Donatello

"I must go retrieve it from down in the cellar," said the barkeep.

"Very well," said Donatello. "But while I wait for the good stuff, I will need a bottle of wine."

The barkeep handed him a wine bottle from behind the bar, then disappeared in the back. Donatello guzzled the wine but spat out a mouthful the moment he glimpsed Lorenzo Ghiberti entering the establishment. Filippo had bested him on a construction project years ago and ever since then, Lorenzo could not help but dwell on that fateful day. From that day on Lorenzo had attributed every failure to being caused by Filippo. His obsession subsumed his vanity and had turned him into a grizzled man focused on revenge. His short hair grew out into a wild, tangled mess. From the corner of his eye, Donatello watched Lorenzo approach two patrons sitting at a table. After a brief conversation, Lorenzo revealed something in a bag, which the patrons signed, then Lorenzo headed over to the bar.

"Donatello?" he asked.

Donatello turned on his barstool. "Do I know you?"

Lorenzo flipped back his matted hair. "It's me, Lorenzo Ghiberti! Remember from back in the day when we were in school together? I heard you were sculpting a masterpiece to go on display beneath my dome."

The words made Donatello chuckle. "Your dome? Well, it must please you that Filippo Brunelleschi is almost done."

The name visibly irked Lorenzo like an exposed nerve in a tooth, and he snapped, "It is still my dome! I had much greater plans to deal with, much greater than that talentless nobody." He managed to recompose himself and asked, "Would you care to contribute to a token of appreciation to be given to the Pope on the day of consecration?"

Donatello finished his waiting wine and opened another bottle. "Will you go away if I do?"

Lorenzo nodded, saying, "If you sign."

Donatello signed his name on a heavy piece of folded cloth, which Lorenzo then took with him.

Chapter Twenty-Six

Born Gabriele Condulmer to a Venetian family of wealth and privilege, Pope Eugene IV ascended to the throne of St. Peter's in 1431 and had to deal with the aftermath of his predecessor's bad judgment and nepotism. The previous pope, Pope Martin V, had accorded lands, positions, wealth, and power to members of his family, the Colonna clan. Upon Martin's death, Pope Eugene aligned himself with the cities of Florence and Venice against Milan and a Colonna-controlled Rome. Fears of an insurgency in Rome led Pope Eugene IV to abscond from the Vatican late one summer night in 1434. Wearing the common robes of a Benedictine monk, he made his way silently to the banks of the Tiber, where an awaiting vessel greeted him. With time being of the essence, they followed the current east, assisted by the rowing of a dozen men. The ship set out to sea, then turned north to follow the Italian coastline until it reached the mouth of the Arno. As the rowers fought the river's current, Pope Eugene IV rejoiced when he laid eyes on the Florentine walls. When his feet touched solid ground, he fell to his knees and led all those around him in prayer for safe passage.

For nearly two years Pope Eugene had been seeking shelter within the city of Florence. From there, he watched as his *condottieri*, or hired mercenaries, recaptured lands and cities from his enemies, either through treaties or bloodshed. Yet Pope Eugene still feared unexpected attacks on his life at all waking moments. While he restlessly slept in his bedchamber behind five locked doors, an entire battalion of soldiers paraded around his quarters at night. He had not lifted anything sharper than a dinner knife since his childhood, but in his late forties he could be seen practicing swordsmanship almost every morning. Despite never suffering an attack, the thought of one kept haunting him, eventually forcing Pope Eugene to relocate his papal entourage to the city of Bologna, which he thought could protect him more ably.

Filippo stepped out of the bright morning light and entered the Santa Maria del Fiore. He stared up at the unfinished canvas above him, yearning for more. "We should postpone everything a week. Okay, maybe a month, seven or eight at the most, so I can finish it."

"You have already accomplished everything you said you were going to do. All those years ago in the Palazzo Vecchio, you never said anything about the inside," said Cosimo behind him. "Your dome has been built. Our beloved cathedral is no longer the world's largest rain well. But above all, you came in under budget and finished within our lifetime. Besides, Pope Eugene will be coming later. Do you know how hard it is to get that hermit to leave the barracks he calls his residence up in Bologna? I'd have better luck getting Piero a nickname like 'the Healthy.' But I wouldn't be surprised if he arrives, throws some water on the wall, makes a cross or two, then leaves before anyone knows he's here."

Filippo looked over his shoulder and asked, "Where's Donatello?"

Cosimo pointed across the interior. "Where else would he be? Probably working on his sculpture."

Elsewhere in the cathedral beyond their vantage point, Donatello examined one of his marble sculptures, the *Cantoria*, hanging on the wall. He had been commissioned to design a singing gallery for the church's choir, but one built earlier by the artist Robbia presented a problem. The church needed more choir space and desired something similar to Robbia's model to complement it. Upon securing the commission, Donatello decided it was more cramped than he had originally thought it would be. He considered his work to be improved plagiarism, no different than his tenure in Rome. The result reflected an extremely large Roman sarcophagus protruding out of carved buttresses from the church wall. The intricate frieze on the exterior showed multiple cherubs dancing, running, and playing between columns. Knowing that the work would be seen in an elevated position, Donatello experimented with aspects of perspective. Yet he was more concerned about whether the workers had attached it securely enough.

Donatello heard Filippo and Cosimo approaching behind him and addressed them without looking away from his work. "I want it in writing, there will be no fat choir singers stepping out on my work. I don't consider it my best, but some obese baritone must not risk destroying it with his gluttony."

"I have told you repeatedly," reminded Filippo, "the workers securely attached it to the wall. It can possibly even support the weight of some of your recent bar conquests."

Cosimo laughed.

"Fine, I'm going to go jump on it," asserted Donatello.

Filippo pointed the way to the choir box, saying, "Please, be my guest," then Cosimo and Filippo exited the cathedral.

In a few minutes Donatello yelled to the empty cathedral, "I'm jumping!" He launched himself up in the air and landed with all his weight. It astonished him that nothing even shook a little. So he reached the logical conclusion and repeatedly jumped up and down in an attempt to bring it down, but it still stood sturdy and attached to the wall.

Donatello wiped off sweat and relented. "Fine, you're right, Filippo. It's sturdy enough to support even the fattest of the fat ones. But I think I need some wine to help unwind from such an intensive test." He listened for a response, but no one called back. "Where did everyone go?" he asked out loud.

As Donatello walked outside into the piazzas around Santa Maria del Fiore, he searched for the first open tavern in sight, but crowds began to gather and impeded his path. With the Pope arriving relatively soon to consecrate the cathedral, all of Florence would be in attendance so no taverns would be open, rationalized Donatello. However, when scouring somewhere to stockpile wine for the occasion, he caught a glimpse of Lorenzo Ghiberti kicking in a locked door to an abandoned building off the piazza and dragging his sack into it. With his curiosity aroused, Donatello decided to forgo the wine and followed Lorenzo.

Outside the building, Donatello looked through the open door to find Lorenzo struggling to drag his bag up the stairs. "Donatello!" he called out. "I could surely use your help!"

Donatello stepped inside the forgotten building. "Sure, I guess."

The two of them fought to get the heavy bag up the first flight of stairs. Traversing the second flight pushed them to near exhaustion. The third and final flight brought them to the brink of death. As they collected their breath at the top, Lorenzo smiled and broke out in uncontrollable laughter. "I'm almost there!"

With great enthusiasm, he kicked open the door to the roof and dragged his bag outside. Donatello followed him out into the sunlight, where the crowds had turned into an endless sea of Florentines walking around the city's streets. "I need just a little more help," said Lorenzo, as he pulled out a canvas tarp folded many times over. When fully unfolded, it stretched nearly the length of the roof. Donatello watched Lorenzo secure a rope through a hole in the canvas and realized that it was a sail from a ship.

"Do me a favor," instructed Lorenzo. "See the openings on the top end? Could you thread some rope through the openings?"

The contingent for Pope Eugene's procession consisted of four dozen soldiers armed with pikes or spears, another two dozen knights on their armored steeds, and a custom-designed papal carriage carrying even more knights on the outside. Inside the carriage's plush velvet interior, an assortment of daggers and hatchets hid behind the decorative façade; Pope Eugene even collaborated with the designer to equip it with a secret compartment that was large enough for him to hide in himself. Despite all these precautions, Pope Eugene felt uneasy outside the confines of Bologna.

When a roaring crowd welcomed him upon arriving in Florence, it made him shrink further into his hand-sewn cushions. After witnessing friends being killed during the chaos of crowded events, he knew it would take just a single moment of inattention for a knife blade to stab him from behind. To ensure his papal longevity as best he could, multiple security committees met almost daily planning his every move for this day. But he still dwelled on the idea of hiding in the secret compartment beneath his seat until he arrived at the cathedral.

The papal procession plodded through Florence very slowly. The armed contingent bored into the clogged streets and created space to advance forward. What should normally have been a quick carriage ride turned into a multi-hour crawl. For Florentines the day marked the civic holiday for the Tuscan New Year. A religious holiday, the Day of Annunciation, which marked the day the angel Gabriel came to the Virgin Mother and informed her of her immaculate conception, also fell on the same day. This holiday was especially important to Florence because the city had been dedicated to the Madonna. Also, for the first time in over five centuries ,Easter had fallen on the same day. When word spread throughout the city that the beloved Santa Maria del Fiore would be consecrated by Pope Eugene IV, all those within Tuscany journeyed far and wide to the city. Never before had Florence seen such crowds.

In the heart of the city, Filippo and Cosimo stood on the steps of the Santa Maria del Fiore with their families behind them. As the papal procession became visible, cheers erupted from the onlookers. However, Filippo's attention turned up to the sky as clouds drifted in front of the sun. Although surrounded by deafening roars, which got louder the closer the procession got, all Filippo could hear were the voices of all his detractors. Only when he recalled his late father's voice did the clouds part, basking Filippo in a radiant light.

Cosimo leaned into the pool of light and spoke to Filippo. "Enjoy this moment, my friend, for you have earned this day like no Florentine before you. You rectified the wretched blight clouding our city. And by doing so, you created something all of Florence will take pride in for all time."

Meanwhile, on a building overlooking the festivities, Donatello finished helping setting up the sail while Lorenzo peered over the edge, watching the papal procession below. "I'm going to drop it down," said Donatello, as he lined up the folded sail on the ledge.

Lorenzo sprinted across the roof and stopped Donatello by screaming, "No! No! No! Now's not the time! I'm so close!"

Donatello backed off and placed his hands up in the air, as Lorenzo reined in his crazy exuberance. "I apologize! What I meant to say was we should wait for the Pope. We don't want to ruin the surprise, now, do we?"

Donatello reluctantly agreed, saying, "If you say so."

"Wonderful," cackled Lorenzo gleefully as he returned to the ledge and waited for the Pope.

With Lorenzo distracted, Donatello silently unraveled the far corner of the sail and read some of the many signatures adorning the fabric. The names were familiar to Donatello and he knew that each of them were critics of Filippo. He unrolled the banner some more and saw much larger script amidst the signatures. Although only a top corner was exposed, he spotted Filippo's name followed by insulting slurs and read more than enough to infer the banner's purpose. Donatello checked to make sure Lorenzo's back was turned, then revealed a small sculpting knife in his palm. He knelt down and cut through the ropes that secured the banner to the roof.

Down below in the piazza the papal procession stopped in front of the Santa Maria del Fiore. Inside the carriage Pope Eugene made the sign of a cross over his chest, kissed a golden cross hanging from his neck, and splashed himself with holy water. "I only have to be out there long enough to do this. I can do this. I am Pope after all," he said to himself in an act of desperate encouragement. Then he reconsidered. "But what if I can't?"

The roaring crowd fell silent waiting for Pope Eugene to make his entrance. Time passed and he still did not appear. On the stairs to the Cathedral, Filippo shrugged his shoulders and looked at Cosimo with a perplexed look on his face. Cosimo whispered back, "The Pope is somewhat agoraphobic and basically thinks everyone's trying to kill him."

Filippo asked, "So, does that make him paranoid or agoraphobic?"

"Who says he can't multitask and do both?" responded Cosimo as the carriage door opened.

Up on the roof, Donatello managed to cut through over half of the ropes when Lorenzo pivoted and frantically said, "Now! Now! The time has come for my revenge!"

Lorenzo pushed the banner off the roof with a gleeful sense of triumph. But then he looked down to discover that the banner, the instrument of his vengeance, was drooping off to a side. He leaned over the edge, grasping at the slouching side while mumbling, "My revenge! I won't let it be like this! I shall have it! I need it!"

Eventually, Pope Eugene rushed out of his carriage and up to the open door of the Santa Maria del Fiore. The impressive sight of Filippo's dome transfixed even Pope Eugene, who forgot his purpose until Cosimo nudged him. "Oh, right, right," he remembered. Turning out to the adoring mass of Florentines, Pope Eugene raised his hands for all to see, then made a cross on the cathedral's door and doused it in holy water.

Donatello emerged from the crowd on the streets and joined the cheering ovation as Pope Eugene went back to the safety of his carriage. However, something caught the Pope's attention. Pointing up at a nearby building, he saw a man suspended in mid-air trying to hang a banner and asked, "Is that man all right?"

Filippo and Cosimo immediately recognized Lorenzo, when a sudden rush of wind blew through the streets of Florence. The powerful gust filled the dropping banner like a windsock and the sheer force of the wind snapped the few ropes restraining the banner to the roof. The entire crowd watched as the wind pushed the banner up through the air, into the sky and out of sight.

Although he never mentioned it to anyone, Filippo knew the wind was a sign of his father's approval for having done the impossible.

Chapter Twenty-Seven

FLORENCE, 1446

In the sixty-eighth year of his life, Filippo Brunelleschi sat up in bed and stretched his arms up into the air. He had spent the past few years designing a lantern to adorn his beloved dome, and later that day the Pope was to consecrate the final construction phase of the Santa Maria. Unlike many, he had the luxury to watch his dreams become a tangible reality, but now as an old man he recognized the constant tribulations such success entailed. The chance to design the lantern was no different, and it had not come easily to Filippo. Many doubted his abilities in the twilight of his career and he had to fight countless other artists for the right to obtain the contract. At first, he worked alongside a younger, somewhat talented artist named Antonio di Ciaccheri Manetti. However, Filippo would eventually come to regret that relationship.

Together, Manetti and Filippo labored day and night designing an engineering marvel to sit on top of the dome. But to the surprise of Filippo and many others, Manetti stole the plans and ideas they had created together, then submitted them as his own work. Feeling betrayed by a friend he had taken under his wing, Filippo relentlessly worked until his hands bled to right the wrong done to him. The sheer thought of some other artist ruining his beloved dome fueled him to succeed. He even resorted to writing his plans in code, using a cipher developed by Julius Caesar. When the contract was finally awarded to Filippo, he proudly accepted it while smiling smugly at Manetti. Many younger artists had hoped to make a name for themselves by besting him and receiving the contract, but Filippo's victory proved that the old lion still reigned supreme in the competitive stone jungle of Florence.

Filippo's award-winning design sought to create a point of convergence at the dome's top extending upward to the sky. His plans called for a white marble coned structure to be the height of five grown men. To help with the weight, eight buttresses would displace it down through the stone spines already supporting the structure. He developed several options but decided on making it appear like a lantern. In his mind, a simple light can provide hope beyond measure to those lost in darkness, and he wanted his work to do the same.

A lifetime spent building the impossible had taught him that the contract signified the start of a journey down a road of countless hiccups and unforeseen impediments. Like years before, the marble would come from the quarries of Carrara. But amassing the quantity of marble Filippo required and its subsequent transport to Florence took much longer than expected. It was during this time that Filippo began to design yet another innovative machine to help ease the burden of construction. With the past complications of the dome still fresh in his mind, he engineered a system composed of multiple pulleys to lift the marble stones into place. Due to the weight, a massive counterweight helped keep the contraption balanced. He also would incorporate a unique braking system by fitting a vertical gear with a ratchet wheel and a pawl that could be locked into place.

∼

Upon arriving at the Santa Maria del Fiore, Filippo saw a moderate-sized crowd gathered to attend the consecration of the lantern. The ceremony was to be performed by Pope Eugene, which Filippo believed gave him more time to arrive at the ceremony. Making his way through the crowd, he was shocked to see the papal carriage already there.

"About time you made it, old friend," said Cosimo, walking through the crowd toward Filippo. "I was worried you had over-slept or forgotten."

Filippo smiled a satisfied smile and said, "I wouldn't have missed this day for the world. If Attila and his Huns stood in my way, I would still find a way to be here. However, I did not expect to be bested in arrival by the Pope, of all people."

"He probably thought all his enemies would still be asleep, so he woke up early," joked Cosimo. "Come, let us find our places as the ceremony should be commencing soon."

From the sidelines they watched Pope Eugene emerge from his golden carriage like a worried squirrel with a falcon circling above him. Pope Eugene approached the first block of marble to be laid and with one hand he splashed a vial of holy water on the stone and made a cross with the other. Then he turned around to an applauding crowd but did not acknowledge them; instead, he hurried back to the confines of his carriage.

Cosimo chortled at the display and said, "The Pope is still frightened by any shadow, his own included. And Filippo, old friend, you are still producing innovative work capable of aston-ishing all who beholds it. Some things never change."

"Let us hope the latter stays that way for quite some time," added a sniffling Filippo.

Cosimo said, "It sounds like you have a slight malady residing within your nose. Would you like me to send my physician for a remedy?"

"Thank you for the kind gesture, but it is nothing but a trifle of a sniffle. I was reviewing some of the construction plans last night and happened to doze off with the window open. The cool breeze may have bothered my nose, but it will take more than mere mucus to dampen my resolve."

Cosimo patted Filippo on the shoulder. "Let me reiterate my earlier statement: some things never change."

That night Filippo toiled until the early morning hours as he had so many times before. Upon reaching an appropriate stopping point, he climbed beneath the sheets on his bed, then turned toward an open window. He briefly entertained the idea of shutting it, but the warmth of his bed prevented him from leaving. As he closed his eyes and entered a deep slumber, a slight breeze blew through the window and made Filippo tighten the blankets around himself.

After being briefly ill, Filippo Brunelleschi suddenly succumbed to his illness on April 15, 1446, in his beloved Florence. The news of his death caused waves of grief over all of Tuscany. Beneath his dome Filippo was laid out and swaddled in white muslin, and thousands and thousands of Florentines came to pay their last respects. When the candles were extinguished, his body was transported to the Giotto's Campanile and a battle waged over what to do with it. One side wanted to see Filippo interred in the Santa Maria del Fiore, while the opposition argued against Filippo even in death. Eventually, Filippo's side would win, and he was buried within the Santa Maria on May 15, 1446.

About the Author

Originally from Georgia, Joe Cline majored in anthropology and minored in history at Southern Methodist University in Dallas, Texas. After working on his master's degree in biological anthropology at Georgia State, he ventured westward to California for more graduate school at Pepperdine University and received his master's degree in fine arts in screenwriting for television and film. His interests include writing (duh), lots of Brazilian Jiu-Jitsu, history, evolutionary theory, primatology, coffee, and his fabled battle cat of lore, Monkeycat.

Dark Labyrinth
A Novel Based on the Life of Galileo Galilei
by Peter David Myers

Defying Danger
A Novel Based on the Life of Father Matteo Ricci
by Nicole Gregory

The Divine Proportions of Luca Pacioli
A Novel Based on the Life of Luca Pacioli
by W. A. W. Parker

Dreams of Discovery
A Novel Based on the Life of the Explorer John Cabot
by Jule Selbo

The Faithful
A Novel Based on the Life of Giuseppe Verdi
by Collin Mitchell

Fermi's Gifts
A Novel Based on the Life of Enrico Fermi
by Kate Fuglei

First Among Equals
A Novel Based on the Life of Cosimo de' Medici
by Francesco Massaccesi

God's Messenger
A Novel Based on the Life of Mother Frances X. Cabrini
by Nicole Gregory

Grace Notes
A Novel Based on the Life of Henry Mancini
by Stacia Raymond

Harvesting the American Dream
A Novel Based on the Life of Ernest Gallo
by Karen Richardson

Humble Servant of Truth
A Novel Based on the Life of Thomas Aquinas
by Margaret O'Reilly

Leonardo's Secret
A Novel Based on the Life of Leonardo da Vinci
by Peter David Myers

Little by Little We Won
A Novel Based on the Life of Angela Bambace
by Peg A. Lamphier, PhD

The Making of a Prince
A Novel Based on the Life of Niccolò Machiavelli
by Maurizio Marmorstein

A Man of Action Saving Liberty
A Novel Based on the Life of Giuseppe Garibaldi
by Rosanne Welch, PhD

Marconi and His Muses
A Novel Based on the Life of Guglielmo Marconi
by Pamela Winfrey

No Person Above the Law
A Novel Based on the Life of Judge John J. Sirica
by Cynthia Cooper

Relentless Visionary: Alessandro Volta
by Michael Berick

Ride Into the Sun
A Novel Based on the Life of Scipio Africanus
by Patric Verrone

Saving the Republic
A Novel Based on the Life of Marcus Cicero
by Eric D. Martin

Soldier, Diplomat, Archaeologist
A Novel Based on the Bold Life of Louis Palma di Cesnola
by Peg A. Lamphier, PhD

The Soul of a Child
A Novel Based on the Life of Maria Montessori
by Kate Fuglei

What a Woman Can Do
A Novel Based on the Life of Artemisia Gentileschi
by Peg A. Lamphier, PhD

For more information on these titles and
the Mentoris Project, please visit
www.mentorisproject.org